Mazirian the Magician

Jack Vance

MAZIRIAN the MAGICIAN

Tales of the Dying Earth, Book I

Published by Spatterlight Press

Cover art by Konstantin Korobov

ISBN 978-161947-402-4

Spatterlight Press LLC

Spatterlight
PRESS

340 S. Lemon Ave #1916
Walnut, CA 91789

www.jackvance.com

Contents

Foreword

Jack Vance would probably not have agreed with me and neither will many of his readers, when I say that *The Dying Earth* sequence is the best he ever wrote. I am not really qualified to make that judgement because I am unfamiliar with much of his SF and am not really a mystery reader. In spite of a considerable difference in our politics, I do tend to think of Jack and his good friend Poul Anderson, in the early flowering of their imaginations, as fellow spirits. Certainly they are two of the few more or less contemporary American writers to whom I can point as direct influences on my own stories. Some of my earliest work was written in homage to their own. Their first imaginative books were works of fantasy published in the 1950s before Tolkien and Howard had come to define the sub-genres of High Fantasy and Sword and Sorcery and *Dungeons and Dragons* laid their ultimately corrosive stereotypes and cliches on our unused dining room tables. *The Dying Earth* came out first, in 1950, from a somewhat obscure publisher, and Abelard-Schuman published Anderson's Norse/Anglo-Saxon epic tale *The Broken Sword* (1954) (itself something of a sequel to Haggard's *Eric Brighteyes*). Both were written well before *The Fellowship of the Ring* was published and bear the sense of vivid discovery common to many early works of fiction not written in the shadow of generic identification.

When, some ten years later, I began writing stories influenced by Anderson and Vance, I was told plainly that there was no book market for that sort of thing and my second Elric book, *Stormbringer,* came out with the letters SF more prominent than Fantasy because booksellers and the public identified 'fantasy' with children's fairy tales. It took the paperbacks of those books to find the growing public taste for supernatural adventure tales exemplified by Lin Carter's Ballantine Adult Fantasy series which eventually reprinted a rather over-civilised version of *The Broken Sword* but did an enormous amount to familiarise modern readers with many of fantastica's great classics. One thing was obvious when *The Dying Earth* eventually took its place beside its peers, this was in no serious sense a derivative work. It had a breath of originality often lacking in his own models. After years of being expensive rarities loaned by one careful fan to another even in the low-priced 1962 Lancer paperback edition done by Vance enthusiast editor and publisher of Elric and Conan, Larry Shaw, *The Dying Earth* began to get the audience it deserved and an enduring place as one of the most admired sequences in fantastic literature. Between them Shaw, the Ballantines, Carter and Donald A. Wollheim did much to start the fantasy renaissance. This sequence was an outstanding addition to the canon.

Many modern authors have claimed Vance as an influence, from Michael Chabon to literary fantast M. John Harrison, whose early Viriconium tales are most strongly redolent of Vance and Clark Ashton Smith. Not being overfamiliar with the Smith/Lovecraft school of fiction, I can't speak for Vance's immediate influences but I am familiar with Smith's. A. C. Swinburne's name is all over the lush, exotic/erotic prose poems of Zothique or Poseidonis. Rivalling Jack's own, Swinburne's unique longevity and facility meant that his poetry became almost wholly identified in the public imagination with the 'greenery-yallery' image of the later Wildean aesthete. Somehow I can't see Jack, the practical man of action, all-American ex-wartime Merchant Marine, slipping into a velvet jacket of an evening while declaiming limpid verse to a group of over-excited listeners. Yet the fact remains Jack was, in *The Dying Earth,* writing in a tradition which was synonymous with a fin-de-siecle decadence identified in Beardsley's drawings or Dowson's *Pierrot of the Minute,* a strong influence on Lord Dunsany's fables or James Branch Cabell's *Jurgen.* It involves a form of literary posturing that allows the reader into the fun and depends on the satirist's knowing wink rather than a clown's pratfall. It is not Jack London or Dashiell Hammett and nor is it *Big Planet* or *The Dragon Masters.* It has another, in my view more profound dimension, an attention to language, to *tone*, which is Vance at his best and something which I suspect he took a special pleasure in creating.

I am not proposing a bit of cheap pseudo-Freudianism here. I am suggesting that the tensions within the work somehow make it superior to anything Jack Vance achieved in a lifetime of high-achievement and which has a special quality only rarely found elsewhere in his work. I think it remains his finest fiction. *The Dying Earth* sequence is in my view unique not because of the influences Jack brought to it, but for the transcendental originality he discovered in a form, making it entirely his own and showing the author to be the far more complex and subtle individual he was hiding behind protective simplifications. That is why I think these stories, the earliest of which have endured for almost eighty years, will sustain a tradition and at the same time prove to be his most enduring and original work.

— Michael Moorcock, Lost Pines, Texas, 2021

I

Mazirian the Magician

DEEP IN THOUGHT, MAZIRIAN THE MAGICIAN walked his garden. Trees fruited with many intoxications overhung his path, and flowers bowed obsequiously as he passed. An inch above the ground, dull as agates, the eyes of mandrakes followed the tread of his black-slippered feet. Such was Mazirian's garden — three terraces growing with strange and wonderful vegetations. Certain plants swam with changing iridescences; others held up blooms pulsing like sea-anemones, purple, green, lilac, pink, yellow. Here grew trees like feather parasols, trees with transparent trunks threaded with red and yellow veins, trees with foliage like metal foil, each leaf a different metal — copper, silver, blue tantalum, bronze, green iridium. Here blooms like bubbles tugged gently upward from glazed green leaves, there a shrub bore a thousand pipe-shaped blossoms, each whistling softly to make music of the ancient Earth, of the ruby-red sunlight, water seeping through black soil, the languid winds. And beyond the roqual hedge the trees of the forest made a tall wall of mystery. In this waning hour of Earth's life no man could count himself familiar with the glens, the glades, the dells and deeps, the secluded clearings, the ruined pavilions, the sun-dappled pleasaunces, the gullies and heights, the various brooks, freshets, ponds, the meadows, thickets, brakes and rocky outcrops.

Mazirian paced his garden with a brow frowning in thought. His step was slow and his arms were clenched behind his back. There was one who had brought him puzzlement, doubt, and a great desire: a delightful woman-creature who dwelt in the woods. She came to his garden half-laughing and always wary, riding a black horse with eyes like golden crystals. Many times had Mazirian tried to take her; always her horse had borne her from his varied enticements, threats, and subterfuges.

Agonized screaming jarred the garden. Mazirian, hastening his step, found a mole chewing the stalk of a plant-animal hybrid. He killed the marauder, and the screams subsided to a dull gasping. Mazirian stroked a furry leaf and the red mouth hissed in pleasure.

Then: "K-k-k-k-k-k-k," spoke the plant. Mazirian stooped, held the rodent to the red mouth. The mouth sucked, the small body slid into the stomach-bladder underground. The plant gurgled, eructated, and Mazirian watched with satisfaction.

The sun had swung low in the sky, so dim and red that the stars could be seen. And now Mazirian felt a watching presence. It would be the woman of the forest, for thus had she disturbed him before. He paused in his stride, feeling for the direction of the gaze.

He shouted a spell of immobilization. Behind him the plant-animal froze to rigidity and a great green moth wafted to the ground. He whirled around. There she was, at the edge of the forest, closer than ever she had approached before. Nor did she move as he advanced. Mazirian's young-old eyes shone. He would take her to his manse and keep her in a prison of green glass. He would test her brain with fire, with cold, with pain and with joy. She should serve him with wine and make the eighteen motions of allurement by yellow lamp-light. Perhaps she was spying on him; if so, the Magician would discover immediately, for he could call no man friend and had forever to guard his garden.

She was but twenty paces distant — then there was a thud and pound of black hooves as she wheeled her mount and fled into the forest.

The Magician flung down his cloak in rage. She held a guard — a counter-spell, a rune of protection — and always she came when he was ill-prepared to follow. He peered into the murky depths, glimpsed the wanness of her body flitting through a shaft of red light, then black shade and she was gone... Was she a witch? Did she come of her own volition, or — more likely — had an enemy sent her to deal him inquietude? If so, who might be guiding her? There was Prince Kandive the Golden, of Kaiin, whom Mazirian had bilked of his secret of renewed youth. There was Azvan the Astronomer, there was Turjan — hardly

Turjan, and here Mazirian's face lit in a pleasing recollection... He put the thought aside. Azvan, at least, he could test. He turned his steps to his workshop, went to a table where rested a cube of clear crystal, shimmering with a red and blue aureole. From a cabinet he brought a bronze gong and a silver hammer. He tapped on the gong and the mellow tone sang through the room and out, away and beyond. He tapped again and again. Suddenly Azvan's face shone from the crystal, beaded with pain and great terror.

"Stay the strokes, Mazirian!" cried Azvan. "Strike no more on the gong of my life!"

Mazirian paused, his hand poised over the gong.

"Do you spy on me, Azvan? Do you send a woman to regain the gong?"

"Not I, Master, not I. I fear you too well."

"You must deliver me the woman, Azvan; I insist."

"Impossible, Master! I know not who or what she is!"

Mazirian made as if to strike. Azvan poured forth such a torrent of supplication that Mazirian with a gesture of disgust threw down the hammer and restored the gong to its place. Azvan's face drifted slowly away, and the fine cube of crystal shone blank as before.

Mazirian stroked his chin. Apparently he must capture the girl himself. Later, when black night lay across the forest, he would seek through his books for spells to guard him through the unpredictable glades. They would be poignant corrosive spells, of such a nature that one would daunt the brain of an ordinary man and two render him mad. Mazirian, by dint of stringent exercise, could encompass four of the most formidable, or six of the lesser spells.

He put the project from his mind and went to a long vat bathed in a flood of green light. Under a wash of clear fluid lay the body of a man, ghastly below the green glare, but of great physical beauty. His torso tapered from wide shoulders through lean flanks to long strong legs and arched feet; his face was clean and cold with hard flat features. Dusty golden hair clung about his head.

Mazirian stared at the thing, which he had cultivated from a single cell. It needed only intelligence, and this he knew not how to provide. Turjan of Miir held the knowledge, and Turjan—Mazirian glanced with a grim narrowing of the eyes at a trap in the floor — refused to part with his secret.

Mazirian pondered the creature in the vat. It was a perfect body; therefore might not the brain be ordered and pliant? He would discover. He set in motion a device to draw off the liquid and presently the body lay stark to the direct rays. Mazirian injected a minim of drug into the neck. The body twitched. The eyes opened, winced in the glare. Mazirian turned away the projector.

Feebly the creature in the vat moved its arms and feet, as if unaware of their use. Mazirian watched intently: perhaps he had stumbled on the right synthesis for the brain.

"Sit up!" commanded the Magician.

The creature fixed its eyes upon him, and reflexes joined muscle to muscle. It gave a throaty roar and sprang from the vat at Mazirian's throat. In spite of Mazirian's strength it caught him and shook him like a doll.

For all Mazirian's magic he was helpless. The mesmeric spell had been expended, and he had none other in his brain. In any event he could not have uttered the space-twisting syllables with that mindless clutch at his throat.

His hand closed on the neck of a leaden carboy. He swung and struck the head of his creature, which slumped to the floor.

Mazirian, not entirely dissatisfied, studied the glistering body at his feet. The spinal coordination had functioned well. At his table he mixed a white potion, and, lifting the golden head, poured the fluid into the lax mouth. The creature stirred, opened its eyes, propped itself on its elbows. The madness had left its face — but Mazirian sought in vain for the glimmer of intelligence. The eyes were as vacant as those of a lizard.

The Magician shook his head in annoyance. He went to the window and his brooding profile was cut black against the oval panes… Turjan once more? Under the most dire inquiry Turjan had kept his secret close. Mazirian's thin mouth curved wryly. Perhaps if he inserted another angle in the passage…

The sun had gone from the sky and there was dimness in Mazirian's garden. His white night-blossoms opened and their captive gray moths fluttered from bloom to bloom. Mazirian pulled open the trap in the floor and descended stone stairs. Down, down, down... At last a passage intercepted at right angles, lit with the yellow light of eternal lamps. To the left were his fungus beds, to the right a stout oak and iron door, locked with three locks. Down and ahead the stone steps continued, dropping into blackness.

Mazirian unlocked the three locks, flung wide the door. The room within was bare except for a stone pedestal supporting a glass-topped box. The box measured a yard on a side and was four or five inches high. Within the box — actually a squared passageway, a run with four right angles — moved two small creatures, one seeking, the other evading. The predator was a small dragon with furious red eyes and a monstrous fanged mouth. It waddled along the passage on six splayed legs, twitching its tail as it went. The other stood only half the size of the dragon — a strong-featured man, stark naked, with a copper fillet binding his long black hair. He moved slightly faster than his pursuer, which still kept relentless chase, using a measure of craft, speeding, doubling back, lurking at the angle in case the man should unwarily step around. By holding himself continually alert, the man was able to stay beyond the reach of the fangs. The man was Turjan, whom Mazirian by trickery had captured several weeks before, reduced in size and thus imprisoned.

Mazirian watched with pleasure as the reptile sprang upon the momentarily relaxing man, who jerked himself clear by the thickness of his skin. It was time, Mazirian thought, to give both rest and nourishment. He dropped panels across the passage, separating it into halves, isolating man from beast. To both he gave meat and pannikins of water.

Turjan slumped in the passage.

"Ah," said Mazirian, "you are fatigued. You desire rest?"

Turjan remained silent, his eyes closed. Time and the world had lost meaning for him. The only realities were the gray passage and the interminable flight. At unknown intervals came food and a few hours rest.

"Think of the blue sky," said Mazirian, "the white stars, your castle Miir by the river Derna; think of wandering free in the meadows."

The muscles at Turjan's mouth twitched.

"Consider, you might crush the little dragon under your heel."

Turjan looked up. "I would prefer to crush your neck, Mazirian."

Mazirian was unperturbed. "Tell me, how do you invest your vat creatures with intelligence? Speak, and you go free."

Turjan laughed, and there was madness in his laughter.

"Tell you? And then? You would kill me with hot oil in a moment."

Mazirian's thin mouth drooped petulantly.

"Wretched man, I know how to make you speak. If your mouth were stuffed, waxed and sealed, you would speak! Tomorrow I take a nerve from your arm and draw coarse cloth along its length."

The small Turjan sitting with his legs across the passageway, drank his water and said nothing.

"Tonight," said Mazirian with studied malevolence, "I add an angle and change your run to a pentagon."

Turjan paused and looked up through the glass cover at his enemy. Then he slowly sipped his water. With five angles there would be less time to evade the charge of the monster, less of the hall in view from one angle.

"Tomorrow," said Mazirian, "you will need all your agility." But another matter occurred to him. He eyed Turjan speculatively. "Yet even this I spare you if you assist me with another problem."

"What is your difficulty, febrile Magician?"

"The image of a woman-creature haunts my brain, and I would capture her." Mazirian's eyes went misty at the thought. "Late afternoon she comes to the edge of my garden riding a great black horse — you know her, Turjan?"

"Not I, Mazirian." Turjan sipped his water.

Mazirian continued. "She has sorcery enough to ward away Felojun's Second Hypnotic Spell — or perhaps she has some protective rune. When I approach, she flees into the forest."

"So then?" asked Turjan, nibbling the meat Mazirian had provided.

"Who may this woman be?" demanded Mazirian, peering down his long nose at the tiny captive.

"How can I say?"

"I must capture her," said Mazirian abstractedly: "What spells, what spells?"

Turjan looked up, although he could see the Magician only indistinctly through the cover of glass.

"Release me, Mazirian, and on my word as a Chosen Hierarch of the Maram-Or, I will deliver you this girl."

"How would you do this?" asked the suspicious Mazirian.

"Pursue her into the forest with my best Live Boots and a headful of spells."

"You would fare no better than I," retorted the Magician. "I give you freedom when I know the synthesis of your vat-things. I myself will pursue the woman."

Turjan lowered his head that the Magician might not read his eyes.

"And as for me, Mazirian?" he inquired after a moment.

"I will treat with you when I return."

"And if you do not return?"

Mazirian stroked his chin and smiled, revealing fine white teeth. "The dragon could devour you now, if it were not for your cursed secret."

The Magician climbed the stairs. Midnight found him in his study, poring through leather-bound tomes and untidy portfolios... At one time a thousand or more runes, spells, incantations, curses, and sorceries had been known. The reach of Grand Motholam — Ascolais, the Ide of Kauchique, Almery to the South, the Land of the Falling Wall to the East — swarmed with sorcerers of every description, of whom the chief was the Arch-Necromancer Phandaal. A hundred spells Phandaal personally had formulated — though rumor said that demons whispered at his ear when he wrought magic. Pontecilla the Pious, then ruler of Grand Motholam, put Phandaal to torment, and after a terrible night, he killed Phandaal and outlawed sorcery throughout the land. The wizards of Grand Motholam fled like beetles under a strong light; the lore was dispersed and forgotten, until now, at this dim time, with the sun dark, wilderness obscuring Ascolais, and the white city Kaiin half in ruins, only a few more than a hundred spells remained to the knowledge of man. Of these, Mazirian had access to seventy-three, and gradually, by stratagem and negotiation, was securing the others.

Mazirian made a selection from his books and with great effort forced five spells upon his brain: Phandaal's Gyrator, Felojun's Second Hypnotic Spell, The Excellent Prismatic Spray, The Charm of Untiring

Nourishment, and the Spell of the Omnipotent Sphere. This accomplished, Mazirian drank wine and retired to his couch.

The following day, when the sun hung low, Mazirian went to walk in his garden. He had but short time to wait. As he loosened the earth at the roots of his moon-geraniums a soft rustle and stamp told that the object of his desire had appeared.

She sat upright in the saddle, a young woman of exquisite configuration. Mazirian slowly stooped, as not to startle her, put his feet into the Live Boots and secured them above the knee.

He stood up. "Ho girl," he cried, "you have come again. Why are you here of evenings? Do you admire the roses? They are vividly red because live red blood flows in their petals. If today you do not flee, I will make you the gift of one."

Mazirian plucked a rose from the shuddering bush and advanced toward her, fighting the surge of the Live Boots. He had taken but four steps when the woman dug her knees into the ribs of her mount and so plunged off through the trees.

Mazirian allowed full scope to the life in his boots. They gave a great bound, and another, and another and he was off in full chase.

So Mazirian entered the forest of fable. On all sides mossy boles twisted up to support the high panoply of leaves. At intervals shafts of sunshine drifted through to lay carmine blots on the turf. In the shade long-stemmed flowers and fragile fungi sprang from the humus; in this ebbing hour of Earth nature was mild and relaxed.

Mazirian in his Live Boots bounded with great speed through the forest, yet the black horse, running with no strain, stayed easily ahead.

For several leagues the woman rode, her hair flying behind like a pennon. She looked back and Mazirian saw the face over her shoulder as a face in a dream. Then she bent forward; the golden-eyed horse thundered ahead and soon was lost to sight. Mazirian followed by tracing the trail in the sod.

The spring and drive began to leave the Live Boots, for they had come far and at great speed. The monstrous leaps became shorter and heavier, but the strides of the horse, shown by the tracks, were also shorter and slower. Presently Mazirian entered a meadow and saw the horse, riderless, cropping grass. He stopped short. The entire expanse of tender herbiage lay before him. The trail of the horse leading into the glade was clear, but there was no trail leaving. The woman therefore had dismounted somewhere behind — how far he had no means of knowing. He walked toward the horse, but the creature shied and bolted through the trees. Mazirian made one effort to follow, and discovered that his Boots hung lax and flaccid — dead.

He kicked them away, cursing the day and his ill-fortune. Shaking the cloak free behind him, a baleful tension shining on his face, he started back along the trail.

In this section of the forest, outcroppings of black and green rock, basalt and serpentine, were frequent — fore-runners of the crags over the River Derna. On one of these rocks Mazirian saw a tiny man-thing mounted on a dragon-fly. He had skin of a greenish cast; he wore a gauzy smock and carried a lance twice his own length.

Mazirian stopped. The Twk-man looked down stolidly.

"Have you seen a woman of my race passing by, Twk-man?"

"I have seen such a woman," responded the Twk-man after a moment of deliberation.

"Where may she be found?"

"What may I expect for the information?"

"Salt — as much as you can bear away."

The Twk-man flourished his lance. "Salt? No. Liane the Wayfarer provides the chieftain Dandanflores salt for all the tribe."

Mazirian could surmise the services for which the bandit-troubadour paid salt. The Twk-men, flying fast on their dragon-flies, saw all that happened in the forest.

"A vial of oil from my telanxis blooms?"

"Good," said the Twk-man. "Show me the vial."

Mazirian did so.

"She left the trail at the lightning-blasted oak lying a little before you. She made directly for the river valley, the shortest route to the lake."

Mazirian laid the vial beside the dragon-fly and went off toward the river oak. The Twk-man watched him go, then dismounted and lashed the vial to the underside of the dragon-fly, next to the skein of fine haft the woman had given him thus to direct Mazirian.

The Magician turned at the oak and soon discovered the trail over the dead leaves. A long open glade lay before him, sloping gently to the river. Trees towered to either side and the long sundown rays steeped one side in blood, left the other deep in black shadow. So deep was the shade that Mazirian did not see the creature seated on a fallen tree; and he sensed it only as it prepared to leap on his back.

Mazirian sprang about to face the thing, which subsided again to sitting posture. It was a Deodand, formed and featured like a handsome man, finely muscled, but with a dead black lusterless skin and long slit eyes.

"Ah, Mazirian, you roam the woods far from home," the black thing's soft voice rose through the glade.

The Deodand, Mazirian knew, craved his body for meat. How had the girl escaped? Her trail led directly past.

"I come seeking, Deodand. Answer my questions, and I undertake to feed you much flesh."

The Deodand's eyes glinted, flitting over Mazirian's body. "You may in any event, Mazirian. Are you with powerful spells today?"

"I am. Tell me, how long has it been since the girl passed? Went she fast, slow, alone or in company? Answer, and I give you meat at such time as you desire."

The Deodand's lips curled mockingly. "Blind Magician! She has not left the glade." He pointed, and Mazirian followed the direction of the dead black arm. But he jumped back as the Deodand sprang. From his mouth gushed the syllables of Phandaal's Gyrator Spell. The Deodand was jerked off his feet and flung high in the air, where he hung whirling, high and low, faster and slower, up to the treetops, low to the ground. Mazirian watched with a half-smile. After a moment he brought the Deodand low and caused the rotations to slacken.

"Will you die quickly or slow?" asked Mazirian. "Help me and I kill you at once. Otherwise you shall rise high where the pelgrane fly."

Fury and fear choked the Deodand.

"May dark Thial spike your eyes! May Kraan hold your living brain in acid!" And it added such charges that Mazirian felt forced to mutter countercurses.

"Up then," said Mazirian at last, with a wave of his hand. The black sprawling body jerked high above the tree-tops to revolve slowly in the crimson bask of setting sun. In a moment a mottled bat-shaped thing with hooked snout swept close and its beak tore the black leg before the crying Deodand could kick it away. Another and another of the shapes flitted across the sun.

"Down, Mazirian!" came the faint call. "I tell what I know."

Mazirian brought him close to earth.

"She passed alone before you came. I made to attack her but she repelled me with a handful of thyle-dust. She went to the end of the glade and took the trail to the river. This trail leads also past the lair of Thrang. So is she lost, for he will sate himself on her till she dies."

Mazirian rubbed his chin. "Had she spells with her?"

"I know not. She will need strong magic to escape the demon Thrang."

"Is there anything else to tell?"

"Nothing."

"Then you may die." And Mazirian caused the creature to revolve at ever greater speed, faster and faster, until there was only a blur. A strangled wailing came and presently the Deodand's frame parted. The head shot like a bullet far down the glade; arms, legs, viscera flew in all directions.

Mazirian went his way. At the end of the glade the trail led steeply down ledges of dark green serpentine to the River Derna. The sun had set and shade filled the valley. Mazirian gained the riverside and set off downstream toward a far shimmer known as Sanra Water, the Lake of Dreams.

An evil odor came to the air, a stink of putrescence and filth. Mazirian went ahead more cautiously, for the lair of Thrang the ghoul-bear was near, and in the air was the feel of magic — strong brutal sorcery his own more subtle spells might not contain.

The sound of voices reached him, the throaty tones of Thrang and gasping cries of terror. Mazirian stepped around a shoulder of rock, inspected the origin of the sounds.

Thrang's lair was an alcove in the rock, where a fetid pile of grass and skins served him for a couch. He had built a rude pen to cage three women, these wearing many bruises on their bodies and the effects of much horror on their faces. Thrang had taken them from the tribe that dwelt in silk-hung barges along the lake-shore. Now they watched as he struggled to subdue the woman he had just captured. His round gray man's face was contorted and he tore away her jerkin with his human hands. But she held away the great sweating body with an amazing dexterity. Mazirian's eyes narrowed. Magic, magic!

So he stood watching, considering how to destroy Thrang with no harm to the woman. But she spied him over Thrang's shoulder.

"See," she panted, "Mazirian has come to kill you."

Thrang twisted about. He saw Mazirian and came charging on all fours, venting roars of wild passion. Mazirian later wondered if the ghoul had cast some sort of spell, for a strange paralysis strove to bind his brain. Perhaps the spell lay in the sight of Thrang's raging gray-white face, the great arms thrust out to grasp.

Mazirian shook off the spell, if such it were, and uttered a spell of his own, and all the valley was lit by streaming darts of fire, lashing in from all directions to spit Thrang's blundering body in a thousand places. This was the Excellent Prismatic Spray — many-colored stabbing lines. Thrang was dead almost at once, purple blood flowing from countless holes where the radiant rain had pierced him.

But Mazirian heeded little. The girl had fled. Mazirian saw her white form running along the river toward the lake, and took up the chase, heedless of the piteous cries of the three women in the pen.

The lake presently lay before him, a great sheet of water whose further rim was but dimly visible. Mazirian came down to the sandy shore and stood seeking across the dark face of Sanra Water, the Lake of Dreams. Deep night with only a verge of afterglow ruled the sky, and stars glistened on the smooth surface. The water lay cool and still, tideless as all Earth's waters had been since the moon had departed the sky.

Where was the woman? There, a pale white form, quiet in the shadow across the river. Mazirian stood on the riverbank, tall and commanding, a light breeze ruffling the cloak around his legs.

"Ho, girl," he called. "It is I, Mazirian, who saved you from Thrang. Come close, that I may speak to you."

"At this distance I hear you well, Magician," she replied. "The closer I approach the farther I must flee."

"Why then do you flee? Return with me and you shall be mistress of many secrets and hold much power."

She laughed. "If I wanted these, Mazirian, would I have fled so far?"

"Who are you then that you desire not the secrets of magic?"

"To you, Mazirian, I am nameless, lest you curse me. Now I go where you may not come." She ran down the shore, waded slowly out till the water circled her waist, then sank out of sight. She was gone.

Mazirian paused indecisively. It was not good to use so many spells and thus shear himself of power. What might exist below the lake? The sense of quiet magic was there, and though he was not at enmity with the Lake Lord, other beings might resent a trespass. However, when the figure of the girl did not break the surface, he uttered the Charm of Untiring Nourishment and entered the cool waters.

He plunged deep through the Lake of Dreams, and as he stood on the bottom, his lungs at ease by virtue of the charm, he marvelled at the fey place he had come upon. Instead of blackness a green light glowed everywhere and the water was but little less clear than air. Plants undulated to the current and with them moved the lake flowers, soft with blossoms of red, blue and yellow. In and out swam large-eyed fish of many shapes.

The bottom dropped by rocky steps to a wide plain where trees of the underlake floated up from slender stalks to elaborate fronds and purple water-fruits, and so till the misty wet distance veiled all. He saw the woman, a white water nymph now, her hair like dark fog. She half-swam half-ran across the sandy floor of the water-world, occasionally looking back over her shoulder. Mazirian came after, his cloak streaming out behind.

He drew nearer to her, exulting. He must punish her for leading him so far...The ancient stone stairs below his work-room led deep and at last opened into chambers that grew ever vaster as one went deeper. Mazirian had found a rusted cage in one of these chambers. A week or two locked in the blackness would curb her willfulness. And once he had dwindled a woman small as his thumb and kept her in a little glass bottle with two buzzing flies...

A ruined white temple showed through the green. There were many columns, some toppled, some still upholding the pediment. The woman entered the great portico under the shadow of the architrave. Perhaps she was attempting to elude him; he must follow closely. The white body glimmered at the far end of the nave, swimming now over the rostrum and into a semi-circular alcove behind.

Mazirian followed as fast as he was able, half-swimming, half-walking through the solemn dimness. He peered across the murk. Smaller columns here precariously upheld a dome from which the keystone had dropped. A sudden fear smote him, then realization as he saw the flash of movement from above. On all sides the columns toppled in, and an avalanche of marble blocks tumbled at his head. He jumped frantically back.

The commotion ceased, the white dust of the ancient mortar drifted away. On the pediment of the main temple the woman kneeled on slender knees, staring down to see how well she had killed Mazirian.

She had failed. Two columns, by sheerest luck, had crashed to either side of him, and a slab had protected his body from the blocks. He moved his head painfully. Through a chink in the tumbled marble he could see the woman, leaning to discern his body. So she would kill him? He, Mazirian, who had already lived more years than he could easily reckon? So much more would she hate and fear him later. He called his charm, the Spell of the Omnipotent Sphere. A film of force formed around his body, expanding to push aside all that resisted. When the marble ruins had been thrust back, he destroyed the sphere, regained his feet, and glared about for the woman. She was almost out of sight, behind a brake of long purple kelp, climbing the slope to the shore. With all his power he set out in pursuit.

T'sain dragged herself up on the beach. Still behind her came Mazirian the Magician, whose power had defeated each of her plans. The memory of his face passed before her and she shivered. He must not take her now.

Fatigue and despair slowed her feet. She had set out with but two spells, the Charm of Untiring Nourishment and a spell affording strength to her arms — the last permitting her to hold off Thrang and tumble the temple upon Mazirian. These were exhausted; she was bare of protection; but, on the other hand, Mazirian could have nothing left.

Perhaps he was ignorant of the vampire-weed. She ran up the slope and stood behind a patch of pale, wind-beaten grass. And now Mazirian came from the lake, a spare form visible against the shimmer of the water.

She retreated, keeping the innocent patch of grass between them. If the grass failed — her mind quailed at the thought of what she must do.

Mazirian strode into the grass. The sickly blades became sinewy fingers. They twined about his ankles, holding him in an unbreakable grip, while others sought to find his skin.

So Mazirian chanted his last spell — the incantation of paralysis, and the vampire grass grew lax and slid limply to earth. T'sain watched with dead hope. He was now close upon her, his cloak flapping behind. Had he no weakness? Did not his fibers ache, did not his breath come short? She whirled and fled across the meadow, toward a grove of black trees. Her skin chilled at the deep shadows, the somber frames. But the thud of the Magician's feet was loud. She plunged into the dread shade. Before all in the grove awoke she must go as far as possible.

Snap! A thong lashed at her. She continued to run. Another and another — she fell. Another great whip and another beat at her. She staggered up, and on, holding her arms before her face. Snap! The flails whistled through the air, and the last blow twisted her around. So she saw Mazirian.

He fought. As the blows rained on him, he tried to seize the whips and break them. But they were supple and springy beyond his powers, and jerked away to beat at him again. Infuriated by his resistance, they concentrated on the unfortunate Magician, who foamed and fought with transcendent fury, and T'sain was permitted to crawl to the edge of the grove with her life.

She looked back in awe at the expression of Mazirian's lust for life. He staggered about in a cloud of whips, his furious obstinate figure dimly silhouetted. He weakened and tried to flee, and then he fell. The blows pelted at him — on his head, shoulders, the long legs. He tried to rise but fell back.

T'sain closed her eyes in lassitude. She felt the blood oozing from her broken flesh. But the most vital mission yet remained. She reached her feet, and reelingly set forth. For a long time the thunder of many blows reached her ears.

Mazirian's garden was surpassingly beautiful by night. The star-blossoms spread wide, each of magic perfection, and the captive half-vegetable moths flew back and forth. Phosphorescent water-lilies floated like charming faces on the pond and the bush which Mazirian had brought from far Almery in the south tinctured the air with sweet fruity perfume.

T'sain, weaving and gasping, now came groping through the garden. Certain of the flowers awoke and regarded her curiously. The half-animal hybrid sleepily chittered at her, thinking to recognize Mazirian's step. Faintly to be heard was the wistful music of the blue-cupped flowers singing of ancient nights when a white moon swam the sky, and great storms and clouds and thunder ruled the seasons.

T'sain passed unheeding. She entered Mazirian's house, found the workroom where glowed the eternal yellow lamps. Mazirian's golden-haired vat-thing sat up suddenly and stared at her with his beautiful vacant eyes.

She found Mazirian's keys in the cabinet, and managed to claw open the trap door. Here she slumped to rest and let the pink gloom pass from her eyes. Visions began to come — Mazirian, tall and arrogant, stepping out to kill Thrang; the strange-hued flowers under the lake; Mazirian, his magic lost, fighting the whips... She was brought from the half-trance by the vat-thing timidly fumbling with her hair.

She shook herself awake, and half-walked, half-fell down the stairs. She unlocked the thrice-bound door, thrust it open with almost the last desperate urge of her body. She wandered in to clutch at the pedestal where the glass-topped box stood and Turjan and the dragon were playing their desperate game. She flung the glass crashing to the floor, gently lifted Turjan out and set him down.

The spell was disrupted by the touch of the rune at her wrist, and Turjan became a man again. He looked aghast at the nearly unrecognizable T'sain.

She tried to smile up at him.

"Turjan — you are free —"

"And Mazirian?"

"He is dead." She slumped wearily to the stone floor and lay limp. Turjan surveyed her with an odd emotion in his eyes.

"T'sain, dear creature of my mind," he whispered, "more noble are you than I, who used the only life you knew for my freedom."

He lifted her body in his arms.

"But I shall restore you to the vats. With your brain I build another T'sain, as lovely as you. We go."

He bore her up the stone stairs.

II

Turjan of Miir

TURJAN SAT IN HIS WORKROOM, legs sprawled out from the stool, back against and elbows on the bench. Across the room was a cage; into this Turjan gazed with rueful vexation. The creature in the cage returned the scrutiny with emotions beyond conjecture.

It was a thing to arouse pity — a great head on a small spindly body, with weak rheumy eyes and a flabby button of a nose. The mouth hung slackly wet, the skin glistened waxy pink. In spite of its manifest imperfection, it was to date the most successful product of Turjan's vats.

Turjan stood up, found a bowl of pap. With a long-handled spoon he held food to the creature's mouth. But the mouth refused the spoon and mush trickled down the glazed skin to fall on the rickety frame.

Turjan put down the bowl, stood back and slowly returned to his stool. For a week now it had refused to eat. Did the idiotic visage conceal perception, a will to extinction? As Turjan watched, the white-blue eyes closed, the great head slumped and bumped to the floor of the cage. The limbs relaxed; the creature was dead.

Turjan sighed and left the room. He mounted winding stone stairs and at last came out on the roof of his castle Miir, high above the river Derna. In the west the sun hung close to old earth; ruby shafts, heavy and rich as wine, slanted past the gnarled boles of the archaic forest to lay on the turfed forest floor. The sun sank in accordance with the old ritual; latter-day night fell across the forest, a soft, warm darkness came swiftly, and Turjan stood pondering the death of his latest creature.

He considered its many precursors: the thing all eyes, the boneless creature with the pulsing surface of its brain exposed, the beautiful female body whose intestines trailed out into the nutrient solution like seeking fibrils, the inverted inside-out creatures... Turjan sighed bleakly. His methods were at fault; a fundamental element was lacking from his synthesis, a matrix ordering the components of the pattern.

As he sat gazing across the darkening land, memory took Turjan to a night of years before, when the Sage had stood beside him.

"In ages gone," the Sage had said, his eyes fixed on a low star, "a thousand spells were known to sorcery and the wizards effected their wills. Today, as Earth dies, a hundred spells remain to man's knowledge, and these have come to us through the ancient books... But there is one called Pandelume, who knows all the spells, all the incantations, cantraps, runes, and thaumaturgies that have ever wrenched and molded space..." He had fallen silent, lost in his thoughts.

"Where is this Pandelume?" Turjan had asked presently.

"He dwells in the land of Embelyon," the Sage had replied, "but where this land lies, no one knows."

"How does one find Pandelume, then?"

The Sage had smiled faintly. "If it were ever necessary, a spell exists to take one there."

Both had been silent a moment; then the Sage had spoken, staring out over the forest.

"One may ask anything of Pandelume, and Pandelume will answer—provided that the seeker performs the service Pandelume requires. And Pandelume drives a hard bargain."

Then the Sage had shown Turjan the spell in question, which he had discovered in an ancient portfolio, and kept secret from all the world.

Turjan, remembering this conversation, descended to his study, a long low hall with stone walls and stone floor deadened by a thick russet rug. The tomes which held Turjan's sorcery lay on the long table of black skeel or were thrust helter-skelter into shelves. These were volumes compiled by many wizards of the past, untidy folios collected by the Sage, leather-bound librams setting forth the syllables of a hundred powerful spells, so cogent that Turjan's brain could know but four at a time.

Turjan found a musty portfolio, turned the heavy pages to the spell the Sage had shown him, the Call to the Violent Cloud. He stared down at the characters and they burned with an urgent power, pressing off the page as if frantic to leave the dark solitude of the book.

Turjan closed the book, forcing the spell back into oblivion. He robed himself with a short blue cape, tucked a blade into his belt, fitted the amulet holding Laccodel's Rune to his wrist. Then he sat down and from a journal chose the spells he would take with him. What dangers he might meet he could not know, so he selected three spells of general application: the Excellent Prismatic Spray, Phandaal's Mantle of Stealth, and the Spell of the Slow Hour.

He climbed the parapets of his castle and stood under the far stars, breathing the air of ancient Earth... How many times had this air been breathed before him? What cries of pain had this air experienced, what sighs, laughs, war shouts, cries of exultation, gasps...

The night was wearing on. A blue light wavered in the forest. Turjan watched a moment, then at last squared himself and uttered the Call to the Violent Cloud.

All was quiet; then came a whisper of movement swelling to the roar of great winds. A wisp of white appeared and waxed to a pillar of boiling black smoke. A voice deep and harsh issued from the turbulence.

"At your disturbing power is this instrument come; whence will you go?"

"Four Directions, then One," said Turjan. "Alive must I be brought to Embelyon."

The cloud whirled down; far up and away he was snatched, flung head over heels into incalculable distance. Four directions was he thrust, then one, and at last a great blow hurled him from the cloud, sprawled him into Embelyon.

Turjan gained his feet and tottered a moment, half-dazed. His senses steadied; he looked about him.

He stood on the bank of a limpid pool. Blue flowers grew about his ankles and at his back reared a grove of tall blue-green trees, the leaves blurring on high into mist. Was Embelyon of Earth? The trees were Earth-like, the flowers were of familiar form, the air was of the same texture... But there was an odd lack to this land and it was difficult to determine. Perhaps it came of the horizon's curious vagueness, perhaps from the blurring quality of the air, lucent and uncertain as water.

Most strange, however, was the sky, a mesh of vast ripples and cross-ripples, and these refracted a thousand shafts of colored light, rays which in mid-air wove wondrous lace, rainbow nets, in all the jewel hues. So as Turjan watched, there swept over him beams of claret, topaz, rich violet, radiant green. He now perceived that the colors of the flowers and the trees were but fleeting functions of the sky, for now the flowers were of salmon tint, and the trees a dreaming purple. The flowers deepened to copper, then with a suffusion of crimson, warmed through maroon to scarlet, and the trees had become sea-blue.

"The Land None Knows Where," said Turjan to himself. "Have I been brought high, low, into a pre-existence or into the after-world?" He looked toward the horizon and thought to see a black curtain raising high into the murk, and this curtain encircled the land in all directions.

The sound of galloping hooves approached; he turned to find a black horse lunging break-neck along the bank of the pool. The rider was a young woman with black hair streaming wildly. She wore loose white breeches to the knee and a yellow cape flapping in the wind. One hand clutched the reins, the other flourished a sword.

Turjan warily stepped aside, for her mouth was tight and white as if in anger, and her eyes glowed with a peculiar frenzy. The woman hauled back on the reins, wheeled her horse high around, charged Turjan, and struck out at him with her sword.

Turjan jumped back and whipped free his own blade. When she lunged at him again, he fended off the blow and leaning forward, touched the point to her arm and brought a drop of blood. She drew back startled; then up from her saddle she snatched a bow and flicked an arrow to the string. Turjan sprang forward, dodging the wild sweep of the sword, seized her around the waist, and dragged her to the ground.

She fought with a crazy violence. He had no wish to kill her, and so struggled in a manner not entirely dignified. Finally he held her helpless, her arms pinioned behind her back.

"Quiet, vixen!" said Turjan, "lest I lose patience and stun you!"

"Do as you please," the girl gasped. "Life and death are brothers."

"Why do you seek to harm me?" demanded Turjan. "I have given you no offense."

"You are evil, like all existence." Emotion ground the delicate fibers of her throat. "If power were mine, I would crush the universe to bloody gravel, and stamp it into the ultimate muck."

Turjan in surprise relaxed his grip, and she nearly broke loose. But he caught her again.

"Tell me, where may I find Pandelume?"

The girl stilled her exertion, twisted her head to stare at Turjan. Then: "Search all Embelyon. I will assist you not at all."

If she were more amiable, thought Turjan, she would be a creature of remarkable beauty.

"Tell me where I may find Pandelume," said Turjan, "else I find other uses for you."

She was silent for a moment, her eyes blazing with madness. Then she spoke in a vibrant voice.

"Pandelume dwells beside the stream only a few paces distant."

Turjan released her, but he took her sword and bow.

"If I return these to you, will you go your way in peace?"

For a moment she glared; then without words she mounted her horse and rode off through the trees.

Turjan watched her disappear through the shafts of jewel colors, then went in the direction she had indicated. Soon he came to a long low manse of red stone backed by dark trees. As he approached the door swung open. Turjan halted in mid-stride.

"Enter!" came a voice. "Enter, Turjan of Miir!"

So Turjan wonderingly entered the manse of Pandelume. He found himself in a tapestried chamber, bare of furnishing save a single settee. No one came to greet him. A closed door stood at the opposite wall, and Turjan went to pass through, thinking perhaps it was expected of him.

"Halt, Turjan," spoke the voice. "No one may gaze on Pandelume. It is the law."

Turjan, standing in the middle of the room, spoke to his unseen host.

"This is my mission, Pandelume," he said. "For some time I have been striving to create humanity in my vats. Yet always I fail, from ignorance of the agent that binds and orders the patterns. This master-matrix must be known to you; therefore I come to you for guidance."

"Willingly will I aid you," said Pandelume. "There is, however, another aspect involved. The universe is methodized by symmetry and balance; in every aspect of existence is this equipoise observed. Consequently, even in the trivial scope of our dealings, this equivalence must be maintained, thus and thus. I agree to assist you; in return, you perform a service of equal value for me. When you have completed this small work, I will instruct and guide you to your complete satisfaction."

"What may this service be?" inquired Turjan.

"A man lives in the land of Ascolais, not far from your Castle Miir. About his neck hangs an amulet of carved blue stone. This you must take from him and bring to me."

Turjan considered a moment.

"Very well," he said. "I will do what I can. Who is the man?"

Pandelume answered in a soft voice.

"Prince Kandive the Golden."

"Ah," exclaimed Turjan ruefully, "you have gone to no pains to make my task a pleasant one... But I will fulfill your requirements as best I can."

"Good," said Pandelume. "Now I must instruct you. Kandive wears this amulet hidden below his singlet. When an enemy appears, he takes it out to display on his chest, such is the potency of the charm. No matter what else, do not gaze on this amulet, either before or after you take it, on pain of most hideous consequence."

"I understand," said Turjan. "I will obey. Now there is a question I would ask — providing the answer will not involve me in an undertaking to bring the Moon back to Earth, or recover an elixir you inadvertently spilled in the sea."

Pandelume laughed loud. "Ask on," he responded, "and I will answer."

Turjan put his question.

"As I approached your dwelling, a woman of insane fury wished to kill me. This I would not permit and she departed in rage. Who is this woman and why is she thus?"

Pandelume's voice was amused. "I, too," he replied, "have vats where I mold life into varied forms. This girl T'sais I created, but I wrought carelessly, with a flaw in the synthesis. So she climbed from the vat with a warp in her brain, in this manner: what we hold to be beautiful seems to her loathsome and ugly, and what we find ugly is to her intolerably vile, in a degree that you and I cannot understand. She finds the world a bitter place, peopled with shapes of direst malevolence."

"So this is the answer," Turjan murmured. "Pitiable wretch!"

"Now," said Pandelume, "you must be on your way to Kaiin; the auspices are good... In a moment open this door, enter, and move to the pattern of runes on the floor."

Turjan performed as he was bid. He found the next room to be circular and high-domed, with the varying lights of Embelyon pouring down through sky-transparencies. When he stood upon the pattern in the floor, Pandelume spoke again.

"Now close your eyes, for I must enter and touch you. Heed well, do not try to glimpse me!"

Turjan closed his eyes. Presently a step sounded behind him. "Extend your hand," said the voice. Turjan did so and felt a hard object placed therein. "When your mission is accomplished, crush this crystal and at once you will find yourself in this room." A cold hand was laid on his shoulder.

"An instant you will sleep," said Pandelume. "When you awake you will be in the city Kaiin."

The hand departed. A dimness came over Turjan as he stood awaiting the passage. The air had suddenly become full of sound: clattering, a tinkling of many small bells, music, voices. Turjan frowned, pursed his lips: A strange tumult for the austere home of Pandelume!

A woman's voice sounded close by.

"Look, O Santanil, see the man-owl who closes his eyes to merriment!"

There was a man's laughter, suddenly hushed. "Come. The fellow is bereft and possibly violent. Come."

Turjan hesitated, then opened his eyes. It was night in white-walled Kaiin, and festival time. Orange lanterns floated in the air, moving as the breeze took them. From the balconies dangled flower chains and cages of blue fireflies. The streets surged with the wine-flushed populace, costumed in a multitude of bizarre modes. Here was a Melantine bargeman, here a warrior of Valdaran's Green Legion, here another of ancient times wearing one of the old helmets. In a little cleared space a garlanded courtesan of the Kauchique littoral danced the Dance of the Fourteen Silken Movements to the music of flutes. In the shadow of a balcony a girl barbarian of East Almery embraced a man blackened and in leather harness as a Deodand of the forest. They were gay, these people of waning Earth, feverishly merry, for infinite night was close at hand, when the red sun should finally flicker and go black.

Turjan melted into the throng. At a tavern he refreshed himself with biscuits and wine; then he made for the palace of Kandive the Golden.

The palace loomed before him, every window and balcony aglow with light. Among the lords of the city there was feasting and revelry. If Prince Kandive were flushed with drink and unwary, reflected Turjan, the task should not be too difficult. Yet, entering boldly, he might be recognized, for he was known to many in Kaiin. So, uttering Phandaal's Mantle of Stealth, he faded from the sight of all men.

Through the arcade he slipped, into the grand salon, where the lords of Kaiin made merry like the throngs of the street. Turjan threaded the rainbow of silk, velour, sateen, watching the play with amusement. On a terrace some stood looking into a sunken pool where a pair of captured Deodands, their skins like oiled jet, paddled and glared; others tossed darts at the spread-eagled body of a young Cobalt Mountain witch. In alcoves beflowered girls offered synthetic love to wheezing old men, and elsewhere others lay stupefied by dream-powders. Nowhere did Turjan find Prince Kandive. Through the palace he wandered, room after room, until at last in an upper chamber he came upon the tall golden-bearded prince, lolling on a couch with a masked girl-child who had green eyes and hair dyed pale green.

Some intuition or perhaps a charm warned Kandive when Turjan slipped through the purple hangings. Kandive leapt to his feet.

"Go!" he ordered the girl. "Out of the room quickly! Mischief moves somewhere near and I must blast it with magic!"

The girl ran hastily from the chamber. Kandive's hand stole to his throat and pulled forth the hidden amulet. But Turjan shielded his gaze with his hand.

Kandive uttered a powerful charm which loosened space free of all warp. So Turjan's spell was void and he became visible.

"Turjan of Miir skulks through my palace!" snarled Kandive.

"With ready death on my lips," spoke Turjan. "Turn your back, Kandive, or I speak a spell and run you through with my sword."

Kandive made as if to obey, but instead shouted the syllables bringing the Omnipotent Sphere about him.

"Now I call my guards, Turjan," announced Kandive contemptuously, "and you shall be cast to the Deodands in the tank."

Kandive did not know the engraved band Turjan wore on his wrist, a most powerful rune, maintaining a field solvent of all magic. Still guarding his vision against the amulet, Turjan stepped through the Sphere. Kandive's great blue eyes bulged.

"Call the guards," said Turjan. "They will find your body riddled by lines of fire."

"*Your* body, Turjan!" cried the Prince, babbling the spell. Instantly the blazing wires of the Excellent Prismatic Spray lashed from all directions at Turjan. Kandive watched the furious rain with a wolfish grin, but his expression changed quickly to consternation. A finger's breadth from Turjan's skin the fire-darts dissolved into a thousand gray puffs of smoke.

"Turn your back, Kandive," Turjan ordered. "Your magic is useless against Laccodel's Rune." But Kandive took a step toward a spring in the wall.

"Halt!" cried Turjan. "One more step and the Spray splits you thousandfold!"

Kandive stopped short. In helpless rage he turned his back and Turjan, stepping forward quickly, reached over Kandive's neck, seized the amulet and raised it free. It crawled in his hand and through the fingers there passed a glimpse of blue. A daze shook his brain, and for an instant he heard a murmur of avid voices... His vision cleared. He backed away from Kandive, stuffing the amulet in his pouch. Kandive asked, "May I now turn about in safety?"

"When you wish," responded Turjan, clasping his pouch. Kandive, seeing Turjan occupied, negligently stepped to the wall and placed his hand on a spring.

"Turjan," he said, "you are lost. Before you may utter a syllable, I will open the floor and drop you a great dark distance. Can your charms avail against this?"

Turjan halted in mid-motion, fixed his eyes upon Kandive's red and gold face. Then he dropped his eyes sheepishly. "Ah, Kandive," he fretted, "you have outwitted me. If I return you the amulet, may I go free?"

"Toss the amulet at my feet," said Kandive, gloating. "Also Laccodel's Rune. Then I shall decide what mercy to grant you."

"Even the Rune?" Turjan asked, forcing a piteous note to his voice.

"Or your life."

Turjan reached into his pouch and grasped the crystal Pandelume had given him. He pulled it forth and held it against the pommel of his sword.

"Ho, Kandive," he said, "I have discerned your trick. You merely wish to frighten me into surrender. I defy you!"

Kandive shrugged. "Die then." He pushed the spring. The floor jerked open, and Turjan disappeared into the gulf. But when Kandive raced below to claim Turjan's body, he found no trace, and he spent the rest of the night in temper, brooding over wine.

Turjan found himself in the circular room of Pandelume's manse. Embelyon's many-colored lights streamed through the sky-windows upon his shoulder — sapphire blue, the yellow of marigolds, blood red. There was silence through the house. Turjan moved away from the rune in the floor, glancing uneasily to the door, fearful lest Pandelume, unaware of his presence, enter the room.

"Pandelume!" he called. "I have returned!"

There was no response. Deep quiet held the house. Turjan wished he were in the open air where the odor of sorcery was less strong. He looked at the doors; one led to the entrance hall, the other he knew not where. The door on the right hand must lead outside; he laid his hand on the latch to pull it open. But he paused. Suppose he were mistaken, and Pandelume's form were revealed? Would it be wiser to wait here?

A solution occurred to him. His back to the door, he swung it open.

"Pandelume!" he called.

A soft intermittent sound came to his ears from behind, and he seemed to hear a labored breath. Suddenly frightened, Turjan stepped back into the circular room and closed the door.

He resigned himself to patience and sat on the floor.

A gasping cry came from the next room. Turjan leapt to his feet.

"Turjan? You are there?"

"Yes; I have returned with the amulet."

"Do this quickly," panted the voice. "Guarding your sight, hang the amulet over your neck and enter."

Turjan, spurred by the urgency of the voice, closed his eyes and arranged the amulet on his chest. He groped to the door and flung it wide.

Silence of a shocked intensity held an instant; then came an appalling screech, so wild and demoniac that Turjan's brain sang. Mighty pinions buffeted the air, there was a hiss and the scrape of metal. Then, amidst muffled roaring, an icy wind bit Turjan's face. Another hiss — and all was quiet.

"My gratitude is yours," said the calm voice of Pandelume. "Few times have I experienced such dire stress, and without your aid might not have repulsed that creature of hell."

A hand lifted the amulet from Turjan's neck. After a moment of silence Pandelume's voice sounded again from a distance.

"You may open your eyes."

Turjan did so. He was in Pandelume's workroom; amidst much else, he saw vats like his own.

"I will not thank you," said Pandelume. "But in order that a fitting symmetry be maintained, I perform a service for a service. I will not only guide your hands as you work among the vats, but also will I teach you other matters of value."

In this fashion did Turjan enter his apprenticeship to Pandelume. Day and far into the opalescent Embelyon night he worked under Pandelume's unseen tutelage. He learned the secret of renewed youth, many spells of the ancients, and a strange abstract lore that Pandelume termed "Mathematics".

"Within this instrument," said Pandelume, "resides the Universe. Passive in itself and not of sorcery, it elucidates every problem, each phase of existence, all the secrets of time and space. Your spells and runes are built upon its power and codified according to a great underlying mosaic of magic. The design of this mosaic we cannot surmise; our knowledge is didactic, empirical, arbitrary. Phandaal glimpsed the pattern and so was able to formulate many of the spells which bear his name. I have endeavored through the ages to break the clouded glass, but so far my research has failed. He who discovers the pattern will know all of sorcery and be a man powerful beyond comprehension."

So Turjan applied himself to the study and learned many of the simpler routines.

"I find herein a wonderful beauty," he told Pandelume. "This is no science, this is art, where equations fall away to elements like resolving chords, and where always prevails a symmetry either explicit or multiplex, but always of a crystalline serenity."

In spite of these other studies, Turjan spent most of his time at the vats, and under Pandelume's guidance achieved the mastery he sought. As a recreation he formed a girl of exotic design, whom he named Floriel. The hair of the girl he had found with Kandive on the night of the festival had fixed in his mind, and he gave his creature pale green hair. She had skin of creamy tan and wide emerald eyes. Turjan was intoxicated with delight when he brought her wet and perfect from the vat. She learned quickly and soon knew how to speak with Turjan. She was one of dreamy and wistful habit, caring for little but wandering among the flowers of the meadow, or sitting silently by the river; yet she was a pleasant creature and her gentle manners amused Turjan.

But one day the black-haired T'sais came riding past on her horse, steely-eyed, slashing at flowers with her sword. The innocent Floriel wandered by and T'sais, exclaiming "Green-eyed woman — your aspect horrifies me, it is death for you!" cut her down as she had the flowers in her path.

Turjan, hearing the hooves, came from the workroom in time to witness the sword-play. He paled in rage and a spell of twisting torment rose to his lips. Then T'sais looked at him and cursed him, and in the pale face and dark eyes he saw her misery and the spirit that caused her to defy her fate and hold to her life. Many emotions fought in him, but at last he permitted T'sais to ride on. He buried Floriel by the riverbank and tried to forget her in intense study.

A few days later he raised his head from his work.

"Pandelume! Are you near?"

"What do you wish, Turjan?"

"You mentioned that when you made T'sais, a flaw warped her

brain. Now I would create one like her, of the same intensity, yet sound of mind and spirit."

"As you will," replied Pandelume indifferently, and gave Turjan the pattern.

So Turjan built a sister to T'sais, and day by day watched the same slender body, and the same proud features take form.

When her time came, and she sat up in her vat, eyes glowing with joyful life, Turjan was breathless in haste to help her forth.

She stood before him wet and naked, a twin to T'sais, but where the face of T'sais was racked by hate, here dwelt peace and merriment; where the eyes of T'sais glowed with fury, here shone the stars of imagination.

Turjan stood wondering at the perfection of his own creation. "Your name shall be T'sain," said he, "and already I know that you will be part of my life."

He abandoned all else to teach T'sain, and she learned with marvellous speed.

"Presently we return to Earth," he told her, "to my home beside a great river in the green land of Ascolais."

"Is the sky of Earth filled with colors?" she inquired.

"No," he replied. "The sky of Earth is a fathomless dark blue, and an ancient red sun rides across the sky. When night falls the stars appear in patterns that I will teach you. Embelyon is beautiful, but Earth is wide, and the horizons extend far off into mystery. As soon as Pandelume wills, we return to Earth."

T'sain loved to swim in the river, and sometimes Turjan came down to splash her and toss rocks in the water while he dreamed. Against T'sais he had warned her, and she had promised to be wary.

But one day, as Turjan made preparations for departure, she wandered far afield through the meadows, mindful only of the colors at play in the sky, the majesty of the tall blurred trees, the changing flowers at her feet; she looked on the world with a wonder that is only for those new from the vats. Across several low hills she wandered, and through a dark forest where she found a cold brook. She drank and sauntered along the bank, and presently came upon a small dwelling.

The door being open, T'sain looked to see who might live here. But the house was vacant, and the only furnishings were a neat pallet of grass, a table with a basket of nuts, a shelf with a few articles of wood and pewter.

T'sain turned to go on her way, but at this moment she heard the ominous thud of hooves, sweeping close like fate. The black horse slid to a stop before her. T'sain shrank back in the doorway, all Turjan's warnings returning to her mind. But T'sais had dismounted and came forward with her sword ready. As she raised to strike, their eyes met, and T'sais halted in wonder.

It was a sight to excite the brain: the beautiful twins, wearing the same white waist-high breeches, with the same intense eyes and careless hair, the same slim pale bodies, the one wearing on her face hate for every atom of the universe, the other a gay exuberance.

T'sais found her voice.

"How is this, witch? You bear my semblance, yet you are not me. Or has the boon of madness come at last to dim my sight of the world?"

T'sain shook her head. "I am T'sain. You are my twin, T'sais, my sister. For this I must love you and you must love me."

"Love? I love nothing! I will kill you and so make the world better by one less evil." She raised her sword again.

"No!" cried T'sain in anguish. "Why do you wish to harm me? I have done no wrong!"

"You do wrong by existing, and you offend me by coming to mock my own hideous mold."

T'sain laughed. "Hideous? No. I am beautiful, for Turjan says so. Therefore you are beautiful, too."

T'sais' face was like marble.

"You make sport of me."

"Never. You are indeed very beautiful."

T'sais dropped the point of her sword to the ground. Her face relaxed into thought.

"Beauty! What is beauty? Can it be that I am blind, that a fiend distorts my vision? Tell me, how does one see beauty?"

"I don't know," said T'sain. "It seems very plain to me. Is not the play of colors across the sky beautiful?"

T'sais looked up in astonishment. "The harsh glarings? They are either angry or dreary, in either case detestable."

"See how delicate are the flowers, fragile and charming."

"They are parasites, they smell vilely."

T'sain was puzzled. "I do not know how to explain beauty. You seem to find joy in nothing. Does nothing give you satisfaction?"

"Only killing and destruction. So then these must be beautiful."

T'sain frowned. "I would term these evil concepts."

"Do you believe so?"

"I am sure of it."

T'sais considered. "How can I know how to act? I have been certain, and now you tell me that I do evil!"

T'sain shrugged. "I have lived little, and I am not wise. Yet I know that everyone is entitled to life. Turjan could explain to you easily."

"Who is Turjan?" inquired T'sais.

"He is a very good man," replied T'sain, "and I love him greatly. Soon we go to Earth, where the sky is vast and deep and of dark blue."

"Earth ... If I went to Earth, could I also find beauty and love?"

"That may be, for you have a brain to understand beauty, and beauty of your own to attract love."

"Then I kill no more, regardless of what wickedness I see. I will ask Pandelume to send me to Earth."

T'sain stepped forward, put her arms around T'sais, and kissed her.

"You are my sister and I will love you."

T'sais' face froze. Rend, stab, bite, said her brain, but a deeper surge welled up from her flowing blood, from every cell of her body, to suffuse her with a sudden flush of pleasure. She smiled.

"Then — I love you, my sister. I kill no more, and I will find and know beauty on Earth or die."

T'sais mounted her horse and set out for Earth, seeking love and beauty.

T'sain stood in the doorway, watching her sister ride off through the colors. Behind her came a shout, and Turjan approached.

"T'sain! Has that frenzied witch harmed you?" He did not wait for a reply. "Enough! I kill her with a spell, that she may wreak no more pain."

He turned to voice a terrible charm of fire, but T'sain put her hand to his mouth.

"No, Turjan, you must not. She has promised to kill no more. She goes to Earth seeking what she may not find in Embelyon."

So Turjan and T'sain watched T'sais disappear across the many-colored meadow.

"Turjan," spoke T'sain.

"What is your wish?"

"When we come to Earth, will you find me a black horse like that of T'sais?"

"Indeed," said Turjan, laughing, as they started back to the house of Pandelume.

III

T'sais

T'SAIS CAME RIDING from the grove. She checked her horse at the verge as if in indecision, and sat looking across the shimmering pastel meadow toward the river... She stirred her knees and the horse proceeded across the turf.

She rode deep in thought, and overhead the sky rippled and cross-rippled, like a vast expanse of windy water, in tremendous shadows from horizon to horizon. Light from above, worked and refracted, flooded the land with a thousand colors, and thus, as T'sais rode, first a green beam flashed on her, then ultramarine, and topaz and ruby red, and the landscape changed in similar tintings and subtlety.

T'sais closed her eyes to the shifting lights. They rasped her nerves, confused her vision. The red glared, the green stifled, the blues and purples hinted at mysteries beyond knowledge. It was as if the entire universe had been expressly designed with an eye to jarring her, provoking her to fury... A butterfly with wings patterned like a precious rug flitted by, and T'sais made to strike at it with her rapier. She restrained herself with great effort; for T'sais was of a passionate nature and not given to restraint. She looked down at the flowers below her horse's feet — pale daisies, blue-bells, Judas-creeper, orange sunbursts. No more would she stamp them to pulp, rend them from their roots. It had been suggested to her that the flaw lay not in the universe but in herself. Swallowing her vast enmity toward the butterfly and the flowers and the changing lights of the sky, she continued across the meadow.

A bank of dark trees rose above her, and beyond were clumps of rushes and the gleam of water, all changing in hue as the light changed in the sky. She turned and followed the river bank to the long low manse.

She dismounted, walked slowly to the door of black smoky wood, which bore the image of a sardonic face. She pulled at the tongue and inside a bell tolled.

There was no reply.

"Pandelume!" she called.

Presently there was a muffled answer: "Enter."

She pushed open the door and came into a high-ceilinged room, bare except for a padded settee, a dim tapestry.

"What is your wish?" The voice, mellow and of an illimitable melancholy, came from beyond the wall.

"Pandelume, today I have learned that killing is evil, and further that my eyes trick me, and that beauty is where I see only harsh light and evil forms."

For a period Pandelume maintained a silence; then the muffled voice came, replying to the implicit plea for knowledge.

"That is, for the most part, true. Living creatures, if nothing else, have the right to life. It is their only truly precious possession, and the stealing of life is a wicked theft... As for the other, the fault is not with you. Beauty lies everywhere free to be seen by all—by all except you. For this I feel sorrow, for I created you. I built your primal cell; I stamped the strings of life with the pattern of your body and brain. And in spite of my craft I erred, so that when you climbed from the vat, I found that I had molded a flaw into your brain; that you saw ugliness in beauty, evil in good. True ugliness, true evil you have never seen, for in Embelyon there is nothing wicked or foul... Should you be so unfortunate to encounter these, I fear for your brain."

"Cannot you change me?" cried T'sais. "You are a magician. Must I live my life out blind to joy?"

The shadow of a sigh penetrated the wall.

"I am a magician indeed, with knowledge of every spell yet devised, the sleight of runes, incantations, designs, exorcisms, talismans. I am Master Mathematician, the first since Phandaal, yet I can do nothing to your brain without destroying your intelligence, your personality, your soul — for I am no god. A god may will things to existence; I must rely on magic, the spells which vibrate and twist space."

Hope faded from T'sais' eyes. "I wish to go to Earth," she said presently. "The sky of Earth is a steady blue, and a red sun moves over the horizons. I tire of Embelyon where there is no voice but yours."

"Earth," mused Pandelume. "A dim place, ancient beyond knowledge. Once it was a tall world of cloudy mountains and bright rivers, and the sun was a white blazing ball. Ages of rain and wind have beaten and rounded the granite, and the sun is feeble and red. The continents have sunk and risen. A million cities have lifted towers, have fallen to dust. In place of the old peoples a few thousand strange souls live. There is evil on Earth, evil distilled by time... Earth is dying and in its twilight..." he paused.

T'sais said doubtfully: "Yet I have heard Earth is a place of beauty, and I would know beauty, even though I die."

"How will you know beauty when you see it?"

"All human beings know beauty... Am I not human?"

"Of course."

"Then I will find beauty, and perhaps even —" T'sais faltered over the word, so alien was it to her mind, yet so full of disturbing implication.

Pandelume was silent. At last:

"You shall go if you wish. I will aid you as I may. I will give you runes to ward you from magic; I will strike life into your sword; and I will give you advice, which is this: Beware of men, for men loot beauty to sate their lust. Permit intimacy to none... I will give you a bag of jewels, which are riches on Earth. With these you may attain much. Yet, again, show them nowhere, for certain men will slay for a copper bit."

A heavy silence came, a weight was gone from the air.

"Pandelume," called T'sais softly. There was no reply.

After a moment Pandelume returned, and the sense of his presence reached to her mind.

"In a moment," he said, "you may enter this room."

T'sais waited a period; then, as she was bid, entered the next room.

"On the bench to the left," came Pandelume's voice, "you will find an amulet and a little sack of gems. Clasp this amulet upon your wrist;

it will reflect magic intended evilly against him who utters the spell. This is a most powerful rune; guard it well."

T'sais obeyed, and tied the jewels inside her sash.

"Lay your sword upon this bench, stand upon the rune in the floor and close your eyes tightly. I must enter the room. I charge you, do not attempt to see me — for there are terrible consequences."

T'sais discarded her sword, stood upon the metal rune, locked her eyes. She heard a slow step, heard the clink of metal, then a high intense shrilling, dying slowly.

"Your sword lives," said Pandelume, and his voice sounded strangely loud, coming from so near. "It will kill your enemies with intelligence. Reach your hand and take it."

T'sais sheathed her slim rapier, now warm and quivering.

"Where on Earth will you go?" asked Pandelume. "To the land of men, or to the great ruined wildernesses?"

"To Ascolais," said T'sais, for the one who had told her of beauty had spoken of this land.

"As you wish," said Pandelume. "Now hark! If you ever seek to return to Embelyon —"

"No," said T'sais. "I would rather die."

"Please yourself in that regard."

T'sais remained silent.

"Now I will touch you. You will be dizzy a moment — and then you will open your eyes on Earth. It is almost night, and terrible things rove the dark. So seek shelter quickly."

In high excitement T'sais felt the touch of Pandelume. There was a wavering in her brain, a swift unthinkable flight... Strange soil was under her feet, strange air at her face with a sharper tang. She opened her eyes.

The landscape was strange and new. There was a dark blue sky, an ancient sun. She stood in a meadow, encircled by tall gloomy trees. These trees were unlike the calm giants of Embelyon; these were dense and brooding, and the shadows were enigmatic. Nothing in sight, nothing of Earth was raw or harsh — the ground, the trees, the rock ledge protruding from the meadow; all these had been worked upon, smoothed, aged, mellowed. The light from the sun, though dim, was rich, and invested every object of the land, the rocks, the trees, the quiet grasses and flowers, with a sense of lore and ancient recollection.

A hundred paces distant rose the mossy ruins of a long tumbled castelry. The stones were blackened now by lichens, by smoke, by age; grass grew rank through the rubble — the whole a weird picture in the long light of sunset.

T'sais slowly approached. Some of the walls yet were standing, stone on weathered stone, the mortar long since dissolved. She moved wonderingly around a great effigy, mouldered, chipped, cracked, almost entirely buried; puzzled a moment at the characters carved in the base. Wide-eyed she stared at what remained of the visage — cruel eyes, sneering mouth, a nose broken off. T'sais shuddered faintly. There was nothing here for her; she turned to go.

A laugh, high-pitched, gleeful, rang across the clearing. T'sais, mindful of Pandelume's warnings, waited in a dark recess. Movement flickered between the trees; and a man and a woman lurched into the failing sunlight; then came a young man treading light as air, singing and whistling. He held a light sword, which he used to prod the two, who were bound.

They halted before the ruins, close by T'sais, and she could see the faces. The bound man was a thin-faced wretch with a ragged red beard and eyes darting and desperate; the woman was short and plump. Their captor was Liane the Wayfarer. His brown hair waved softly, his features moved in charm and flexibility. He had golden-hazel eyes, large and beautiful, never still. He wore red leather shoes with curled tops, a suit of red and green, a green cloak, and a peaked hat with a red feather.

T'sais watched without comprehension. The three were equally vile, of sticky blood, red pulp, inner filth. Liane seemed slightly less ignoble — he was the most agile, the most elegant. And T'sais watched with little interest.

Liane deftly threw loops around the ankles of man and woman and pushed them so that they fell among the flints. The man groaned softly, the woman fell to whimpering.

Liane made a gay flourish of his hat and sprang away to the ruins. Not twenty feet from T'sais he slid aside a stone in the ancient flags, came forth with tinder and flint, and kindled a fire. From his pouch he took a bit of meat, which he toasted and ate daintily, sucking his fingers.

No word had yet passed. Liane at last stood up, stretched, and glanced at the sky. The sun was dropping below the dark wall of trees, and already blue shadows filled the glade.

"To business," cried Liane. His voice was shrill and clear as the call of a flute. "First," and he made a solemnly waggish gesture, "I must assure that our revelations are weighted with soberness and truth."

He ducked into his lair under the flags and brought forth four stout staffs. He laid one of these across the thighs of the man, passed the second across this, through the crotch of his captive's legs, so that with slight effort he could crush down at the thighs and up at the small of the back. He tested his device and crowed as the man cried out. He adjusted a similar arrangement upon the woman.

T'sais watched in perplexity. Evidently the young man was preparing to cause his captives pain. Was this a custom of Earth? But how was she to judge, she who knew nothing of good or evil?

"Liane! Liane!" cried the man. "Spare my wife! She knows nothing! Spare her, and you may have all I possess, and I serve you my lifetime!"

"Ho!" laughed Liane, and the feather of his cap quivered. "Thank you, thank you for your offer — but Liane wants no faggots of wood, no turnips. Liane likes silk and gold, the gleam of daggers, the sounds a girl makes in love. So thank you — but I seek the brother of your wife, and when your wife chokes and screams, you will tell where he hides."

To T'sais the scene began to assume meaning. The two captives were concealing information the young man desired; hence he would hurt them until in desperation they did as he asked. A clever artifice, one which she would hardly have thought of herself.

"Now," said Liane, "I must ensure that lies are not artfully mingled into the truth. You see," he confided, "when one is under torment, he is too distraught to invent, to fabricate — and hence speaks naught but exactness." He snatched a brand from the fire, wedged it between the man's bound ankles, and instantly leapt to ply the torture lever upon the woman.

"I know nothing, Liane!" babbled the man. "I know nothing — oh, indeed!"

Liane stood away with dissatisfaction. The woman had fainted. He snatched the brand away from the man and flung it pettishly into the blaze.

"What a nuisance!" he said, but presently his good spirits reasserted themselves. "Ah well, we have much time." He stroked his pointed chin.

"Perhaps you speak truth," he mused. "Perhaps your good wife shall be the informant after all." He revived her with slaps and an aromatic which he held under her nose. She stared at him numbly, her face twisted and bloated.

"Attend," said Liane. "I enter the second phase of the question. I reason, I think, I theorize. I say, perhaps the husband does not know where he whom I seek has fled, perhaps the wife alone knows."

The woman's mouth opened slightly. "He is my brother — please —"

"Ah! So you know!" cried Liane in delight, and strode back and forth before the fire. "Ah, you know! We renew the trial. Now attend. With this staff I make jelly of your man's legs, and bring his spine up through his stomach — unless you speak."

He set about his task.

"Say nothing —" gasped the man, and lapsed into pain. The woman cursed, sobbed, pleaded. At last: "I tell, I tell you all!" she cried. "Dellare has gone to Efred!"

Liane relaxed his efforts. "Efred. So. In the Land of the Falling Wall." He pursed his lips. "It might be true. But I disbelieve. You must tell me once more, under the influence of the truth-evoker." And he brought a brand from the fire and adjusted it at her ankles — and set to work on the man once more. The woman spoke not.

"Speak, woman," snarled Liane, panting. "I am in perspiration with this work." The woman spoke not. Her eyes were wide, and stared glassily upwards.

"She is dead!" cried her husband. "Dead! My wife is dead! Ah — Liane, you demon, you foulness!" he screamed. "I curse you! by Thial, by Kraan —" His voice quavered into high-pitched hysteria.

T'sais was disturbed. The woman was dead. Was not killing wicked? So Pandelume had said. If the woman were good, as the bearded man had said, then Liane was evil. Things of blood and filth all, of course. Still, it was vile, hurting a live thing till it died.

Knowing nothing of fear, she stepped out from her hiding place and advanced into the fire-light. Liane looked up and sprang back. But the intruder was a slender girl of passionate beauty. He caroled, he danced.

"Welcome, welcome!" He glared in distaste at the bodies on the ground. "Unpleasant; we must ignore them." He flung his cloak back, ogled her with his luminous hazel eyes, strutted toward her like a plumed cock.

"You are lovely, my dear, and I — I am the perfect man; so you shall see."

T'sais laid her hand on her rapier, and it sprang out by itself. Liane leapt back, alarmed by the blade and likewise by the blaze which glowed deep from the warped brain.

"What means this? Come, come," he fretted. "Put away your steel. It is sharp and hard. You must lay it away. I am a kind man, but I brook no annoyance."

T'sais stood over the prone bodies. The man looked up at her feverishly. The woman stared at the dark sky.

Liane sprang forward, planning to clasp her while her attention was distracted. The rapier sprang up by itself, darted forward, pierced the agile body.

Liane the Wayfarer sank to his knees coughing blood. T'sais pulled away the rapier, wiped the blood on the gay green cloak, and sheathed it with difficulty. It wished to stab, to pierce, to kill.

Liane lay unconscious. T'sais turned away, sick. A thin voice reached her. "Release me —"

T'sais considered, then she cut the bonds. The man stumbled to his wife, stroked her, flung off the bonds, called to her uplifted face. There was no answer. He sprang erect in madness and howled into the night. Raising the limp form in his arms he stumbled off into the darkness, lurching, falling, cursing…

T'sais shivered. She glanced from the prone Liane to the black forest where the flickering circle of the firelight failed to reach. Slowly, with many backward glances, she left the tumbled ruins, the meadow. The bleeding figure of Liane remained by the dying fire.

The glimmer of flame waned, was lost in the darkness. T'sais groped her way between the looming trunks; and the murk was magnified by the twist in her brain. There never had been night in Embelyon, only an opalescent dimming. So T'sais continued down the sighing forest courses, stifled, weighed, yet oblivious to the things she might have met — the Deodands, the pelgrane, the prowling erbs (creatures mixed of beasts, man and demon), the gids, who leapt twenty feet across the turf and clasped themselves to their victims.

T'sais went unmolested, and presently reached the edge of the forest. The ground rose, the trees thinned, and T'sais came out on an illimitable dark expanse. This was Modavna Moor, a place of history, a tract which had borne the tread of many feet and absorbed much blood. At one famous slaughtering, Golickan Kodek the Conqueror had herded here the populations of two great cities, G'Vasan and Bautiku, constricted them in a circle three miles across, gradually pushed them tighter, tighter, tighter, panicked them toward the center within his flapping-armed sub-human cavalry, until at last he had achieved a gigantic squirming mound, half a thousand feet high, a pyramid of screaming flesh. It is said that Golickan Kodek mused ten minutes at his monument, then turned and rode his bounding mount back to the land of Laidenur from whence he had come.

The ghosts of the ancient populations had paled and dissolved and Modavna Moor was less stifling than the forest. Bushes grew like blots from the ground. A line of rocky crags at the horizon jutted sharp against a faint violet after-glow. T'sais picked her way across the turf, relieved that the sky was open above. A few minutes later she came to an ancient road of stone slab, cracked and broken, bordered by a ditch where luminous star-shaped flowers grew. A wind came sighing off the moor to dampen her face with mist. She went wearily down the road. No shelter was visible, and the wind whipped coldly at her cloak.

A rush of feet, a tumble of shapes, and T'sais was struggling against hard grasping hands. She fought for her rapier, but her arms were pinioned.

One struck a light, fired a torch, to examine his prize. T'sais saw three bearded, scarred rogues of the moor; they wore gray pandy-suits, stained and fouled by mud and filth.

"Why it's a handsome maid!" said one, leering.

"I'll seek about her for silver," said another and slid his hands with evil intimacy over T'sais' body. He found the sack of jewels, and turned them into his palm, a trickle of hundred-colored fire. "Mark these! The wealth of princes!"

"Or sorcerers!" said another. And in sudden doubt they relaxed their holds. But still she could not reach her rapier.

"Who are you, woman of the night?" asked one with some respect. "A witch, to have such jewels, and walk Modavna Moor alone?"

T'sais had neither wit nor experience to improvise falsehood.

"I am no witch! Release me, you stinking animals!"

"No witch? Then what manner of woman are you? Whence do you come?"

"I am T'sais, of Embelyon," she cried angrily. "Pandelume created me, and I seek love and beauty on Earth. Now drop your hands, for I would go my way!"

The first rogue chortled. "Ho, ho! Seeking love and beauty! You have achieved something of your quest, girl — for while we lads are no beauties, to be sure, Tagman being covered with scab and Lasard lacking his teeth and ears — still we have much love, hey, lads? We will show you as much love as you desire! Hey, lads?"

And in spite of T'sais' horrified outcries, they dragged her across the moor to a stone cabin.

They entered, and one kindled a roaring fire, while two stripped T'sais of her rapier and flung it in a corner. They locked the door with a great iron key, and released her. She sprang for her sword, but a buffet sent her to the foul floor.

"May that quiet you, fiend-cat!" panted Tagman. "You should be happy," and they renewed their banter. "Admitted we are not beauties, yet we will show you all the love you may wish."

T'sais crouched in a corner. "I know not what love is," she panted. "In any event I want none of yours!"

"Is it possible?" they crowed. "You are yet innocent?" And T'sais listened with eyes glazing as they proceeded to describe in evil detail their concept of love.

T'sais sprang from her corner in a frenzy, kicking, beating her fists at the moor-men. And when she had been flung into her corner, bruised and half-dead, the men brought out a great cask of mead, to fortify themselves for their pleasure.

Now they cast lots as to who should be the first to enjoy the girl. The issue was declared, and here an altercation arose, two claiming that he who won had cheated. Angry words evolved, and as T'sais watched, dazed in horror beyond the concept of a normal mind, they fought like bulls in a rut, with great curses, mighty blows. T'sais crept to her rapier, and as it felt her touch, it lofted into the air like a bird. It lunged itself into the fight, dragging T'sais behind. The three shouted hoarsely, the steel flickered — in, out, faster than the eye. Cries, groans — and three sprawled on the earthen floor, gaping-mouthed corpses. T'sais found the key, unlocked the door, fled madly through the night.

She ran over the dark and windy moor, across the road, stumbled into the ditch, dragged herself up the cold muddy bank and sank on her knees... This was Earth! She remembered Embelyon, where the most evil things were flowers and butterflies. She remembered how these had aroused her hate.

Embelyon was lost, renounced. And T'sais wept.

A rustling in the heather aroused her. Aghast she lifted her head, listened. What new outrage to her mind? The sinister sounds again, as of cautious footfalls. She searched the darkness in terror.

A black figure stole into her sight, creeping along the ditch. In the light of the fireflies she saw him — a Deodand, wandered from the forest, a hairless man-thing with charcoal-black skin, a handsome face, marred and made demoniac by two fangs gleaming long, sharp and white down his lip. It was clad in a leather harness, and its long slit eyes were fastened hungrily on T'sais. He sprang at her with an exulting cry.

T'sais stumbled clear, fell, snatched herself up. Wailing, she fled across the moor, insensible to scratching furze, tearing thorn. The Deodand bounded after, venting eerie moans.

Over moor, turf, hummock, briar and brook, across the dark wastes went the chase, the girl fleeing with eyes starting and staring into nothing, the pursuer uttering his wistful moans.

A loom, a light ahead — a cottage. T'sais, breath coming in sobs, lurched to the threshold. The door mercifully gave. She fell in, slammed the door, dropped the bar. The weight of the Deodand thudded against the barrier.

The door was stout, the windows small and crossed by iron. She was safe. She sank to her knees, the breath rasping in her throat, and slowly lapsed into unconsciousness...

The man who dwelt in the cottage rose from his deep seat at the fire, tall, broad of shoulder, moving with a curiously slow step. He was perhaps a young man, but no one could know, for his face and head were draped in a black hood. Behind the eye-slits were steady blue eyes.

The man came to stand over T'sais, who lay flung like a doll on the red brick floor. He stooped, lifted the limp form, and carried her to a wide padded bench beside the fire. He removed her sandals, her quivering rapier, her sodden cloak. He brought unguent and applied it to her scratches and bruises. He wrapped her in soft flannel blanketing, pillowed her head, and assured that she was comfortable, once more sat himself by the fire.

The Deodand outside had lingered, and had been watching through the iron-barred window. Now it knocked at the door.

"Who's there?" called the man in the black hood, twisting about.

"I desire the one who has entered. I hunger for her flesh," said the soft voice of the Deodand.

The man in the hood spoke sharply.

"Go, before I speak a spell to burn you with fire. Never return!"

"I go," said the Deodand, for he greatly feared magic, and departed into the night.

And the man turned and sat staring into the fire.

T'sais felt warm pungent liquid in her mouth and opened her eyes. Kneeling beside her was a tall man, hooded in black. One arm supported her shoulders and head, another held a silver spoon to her mouth.

T'sais shrank away. "Quietly," said the man. "Nothing will harm you." Slowly, doubtfully, she relaxed and lay still.

Red sunlight poured in through the windows, and the cottage was warm. It was paneled in golden wood, with a fretwork painted in red and blue and brown circling the ceiling. Now the man brought more broth from the fire, bread from a locker, and placed them before her. After a moment's hesitation, T'sais ate.

Recollection suddenly came to her; she shuddered, looked wildly around the room. The man noted her taut face. He stooped and laid a hand on her head. T'sais lay quiet, half in dread.

"You are safe here," said the man. "Fear nothing."

A vagueness came over T'sais. Her eyes grew heavy. She slept.

When she woke the cottage was empty, and the maroon sunlight slanted in from an opposite window. She stretched her arms, tucked her hand behind her head, and lay thinking. This man of the black hood, who was he? Was he evil? Everything else of Earth had been past thought. Still, he had done nothing to harm her... She spied her garments upon the floor. She rose from the couch and dressed herself. She went to the door and pushed it open. Before her stretched the moor, fading far off beyond the under-slant of the horizon. To her left jutted a break of rocky crags, black shadow and lurid red stones. To the right extended the black margin of the forest.

Was this beautiful? T'sais pondered. Her warped brain saw bleakness in the line of the moor, cutting harshness in the crags, and in the forest — terror.

Was this beauty? At a loss, she twisted her head, squinted. She heard footsteps, jerked about, wide-eyed, expecting anything. It was he of the black hood, and T'sais leaned back against the door-jamb.

She watched him approach, tall and strong, slow of step. Why did he wear the hood? Was he ashamed of his face? She could understand something of this, for she herself found the human face repellent — an object of watery eye, wet unpleasant apertures, spongy outgrowths.

He halted before her. "Are you hungry?"

T'sais considered. "Yes."

"Then we will eat."

He entered the cottage, stirred up the fire, and spitted meat. T'sais stood uncertainly in the background. She had always served herself. She felt an uneasiness: co-operation was an idea she had not yet encountered.

Presently the man arose, and they sat to eat at his table.

"Tell me of yourself," he said after a few moments. So T'sais, who had never learned to be other than artless, told him her story, thus:

"I am T'sais. I came to Earth from Embelyon, where the wizard Pandelume created me."

"Embelyon? Where is Embelyon? And who is Pandelume?"

"Where is Embelyon?" she repeated in puzzlement. "I don't know. It is in a place that is not Earth. It is not very large, and lights of many colors come from the sky. Pandelume lives in Embelyon. He is the greatest wizard alive — so he tells me."

"Ah," the man said. "Perhaps I see..."

"Pandelume created me," continued T'sais, "but there was a flaw in the pattern." And T'sais stared in to the fire. "I see the world as a dismal place of horror; all sounds to me are harsh, all living creatures vile, in varying degrees — things of sluggish movement and inward filth. During the first of my life I thought only to trample, crush, destroy. I knew nothing but hate. Then I met my sister T'sain, who is as I without the flaw. She told me of love and beauty and happiness — and I came to Earth seeking these."

The grave blue eyes studied her.

"Have you found them?"

"So far," said T'sais in a faraway voice, "I have found only such evil as I never even encountered in my nightmares." Slowly she told him her adventures.

"Poor creature," he said and fell to studying her once again.

"I think I shall kill myself," said T'sais, in the same distant voice, "for what I want is infinitely lost." And the man, watching, saw how the red afternoon sun coppered her skin, noted the loose black hair, the long thoughtful eyes. He shuddered at the thought of this creature being lost into the dust of Earth's forgotten trillions.

"No!" he said sharply. T'sais stared at him in surprise. Surely one's life was one's own, to do with as one pleased.

"Have you found nothing on Earth," he asked, "that you would regret leaving?"

T'sais knit her brows. "I can think of nothing — unless it be the peace of this cottage."

The man laughed. "Then this shall be your home, for as long as you wish, and I will try to show you that the world is sometimes good — though in truth —" his voice changed "— I have not found it so."

"Tell me," said T'sais, "what is your name? Why do you wear the hood?"

"My name? Etarr," he said in a voice subtly harsh. "Etarr is enough of it. I wear the mask because of the most wicked woman of Ascolais — Ascolais, Almery, Kauchique — the entire world. She made my face such that I cannot abide my own sight."

He relaxed, and gave a weary laugh. "No need for anger any more."

"Is she alive still?"

"Yes, she lives, and no doubt still works evil on all she meets." He sat looking into the fire. "One time I knew nothing of this. She was young, beautiful, laden with a thousand fragrances and charming playfulnesses. I lived beside the ocean — in a white villa among poplar trees. Across Tenebrosa Bay the Cape of Sad Remembrance reached into the ocean, and when sunset made the sky red and the mountains black, the cape seemed to sleep on the water like one of the ancient earth-gods… All my life I spent here, and was as content as one may be while dying Earth spins out its last few courses.

"One morning I looked up from my star-charts and saw Javanne walking through the portal. She was as young and slender as yourself. Her hair was a wonderful red, and strands fell before her shoulders. She was very beautiful, and — in her white gown — pure and innocent.

"I loved her, and she said she loved me. And she gave me a band of black metal to wear. In my blindness I clasped it to my wrist, never recognizing it for the evil rune it was. And weeks of great delight passed. But presently I found that Javanne was one of dark urges that the love of man could never quell. And one midnight I found her in the embrace of a black naked demon, and the sight twisted my mind.

"I stood back aghast. I was not seen, and I went slowly away. In the morning she came running across the terrace smiling and happy, like a child. 'Leave me,' I told her. 'You are vile beyond calculation.' She uttered a word and the rune on my arm enslaved me. My mind was my own, but my body was hers, forced to obey her words.

"And she made me tell what I had seen, and she revelled and jeered. And she put me through foul degradations, and called up things from Kalu, from Fauvune, from Jeldred, to mock and defile my body. She made me witness her play with these things, and when I pointed out the creature that sickened me the most, by magic she gave me its face, the face I wear now."

"Can such women exist?" marvelled T'sais.

"Indeed." The grave blue eyes studied her attentively. "At last one night while the demons tumbled me across the crags behind the hills, a flint tore the rune from my arm. I was free; I chanted a spell which sent the shapes shrieking off through the sky, and returned to the villa.

"And I met Javanne of the red hair in the great hall, and her eyes were cool and innocent. I drew my knife to stab her throat, but she said, 'Hold! Kill me and you wear your demon-face forever, for only I know how to change it.' So she ran blithely away from the villa, and I, unable to bear the sight of the place, came to the moors. And always I seek her, to regain my face."

"Where is she now?" asked T'sais, whose troubles seemed small compared to those of Etarr the Masked.

"Tomorrow night, I know where to find her. It is the night of the Black Sabbath — the night dedicated to evil since the dawn of Earth."

"And you will attend this festival?"

"Not as a celebrant — though in truth," said Etarr ruefully, "without my hood I would be one of the things who are there, and would pass unnoticed."

T'sais shuddered and pressed back against the wall. Etarr saw the gesture and sighed.

Another idea occurred to her. "With all the evil you have suffered, do you still find beauty in the world?"

"To be sure," said Etarr. "See how these moors stretch, sheer and clean, of marvellous subtle color. See how the crags rise in grandeur, like the spine of the world. And you," he gazed into her face, "you are of a beauty surpassing all."

"Surpassing Javanne?" asked T'sais, and looked in puzzlement as Etarr laughed.

"Indeed surpassing Javanne," he assured her.

T'sais' brain went off at another angle.

"And Javanne, do you wish to revenge yourself against her?"

"No," answered Etarr, eyes far away across the moors. "What is revenge? I care nothing for it. Soon, when the sun goes out, men will stare into the eternal night, and all will die, and Earth will bear its history, its ruins, the mountains worn to knolls — all into infinite dark. Why revenge?"

Presently they left the cottage and wandered across the moor, Etarr trying to show her beauty — the slow river Scaum flowing through green rushes, clouds basking in the wan sunlight over the crags, a bird wheeling on spread wings, the wide smoky sweep of Modavna Moor. And T'sais strove always to make her brain see this beauty, and always did she fail. But she had learned to check the wild anger that the sights of the world had once aroused. And her craving to kill diminished, and her face relaxed from its tense set.

So they wandered on, each to his own thoughts. And they watched the sad glory of the sunset, and they saw the slow white stars rise in the heavens.

"Are not the stars beautiful?" whispered Etarr through his black hood. "They have names older than man."

And T'sais, finding only mournfulness in the sunset, and thinking the stars but small sparks in meaningless patterns could not answer.

"Surely two more unfortunate people do not exist," she sighed.

Etarr said nothing. They walked on in silence. Suddenly he grasped her arm and pulled her low in the furze. Three great shapes went flapping across the afterglow. "The pelgrane!"

They flew close overhead — gargoyle creatures, with wings creaking like rusty hinges. T'sais caught a glimpse of hard leathern body, great hatchet beak, leering eyes in a wizened face. She shrank against Etarr. The pelgrane flapped across the forest.

Etarr laughed harshly. "You shrink from the visage of the pelgrane. The countenance I wear would put the pelgrane themselves to flight."

The next morning he took her into the woods, and she found the trees mindful of Embelyon. They returned to the cottage in the early afternoon, and Etarr retired to his books.

"I am no sorcerer," he told her regretfully. "I am acquainted with but a few simple spells. Yet I make occasional use of magic, which may ward me from danger tonight."

"Tonight?" T'sais inquired vaguely, for she had forgotten.

"Tonight is the Black Sabbath, and I must go to find Javanne."

"I would go with you," said T'sais. "I would see the Black Sabbath, and Javanne also."

Etarr assured her that the sights and sounds would horrify her and torment her brain. T'sais persisted, and Etarr finally allowed her to follow him, when two hours after sunset he set off in the direction of the crags.

Over the heath, up scaly outcroppings, Etarr picked a way through the dark, with T'sais a slender shadow behind. A great scarp lay across their path. Into a black fissure, up a flight of stone steps, cut in the immemorial past, and out on top of the cliff, with Modavna Moor a black sea below.

Now Etarr gestured T'sais to great caution. They stole through a gap between two towering rocks; concealed in the shadow, they surveyed the congress below.

They were overlooking an amphitheater lit by two blazing fires. In the center rose a dais of stone, as high as a man. About the fire, about the dais, two-score figures, robed in gray monks-cloth, reeled sweatingly, their faces unseen.

T'sais felt a premonitory chill. She looked at Etarr doubtfully.

"Even here is beauty," he whispered. "Weird and grotesque, but a sight to enchant the mind." T'sais looked again in dim comprehension. More of the robed and cowled figures now were weaving before the fires; whence they came T'sais had not observed. It was evident that the festival had just begun, that the celebrants were only marshalling their passions.

They pranced, shuffled, wove in and out, and presently began a muffled chant.

The weaving and gesticulation became feverish, and the caped figures crowded more closely around the dais. And now one leapt up on the dais and doffed her robe — a middle-aged witch of squat naked body with a great broad face. She had ecstatic glittering eyes, large features pumping in ceaseless idiotic motion. Mouth open, tongue protruding, stiff black hair like a furze bush, falling from side to side over her face as she shook her head, she danced a libidinous sidelong dance in the light of the fires, looking slyly over the gathering. The chant of the cavorting figures below swelled to a vile chorus, and overhead dark shapes appeared, settling with an evil sureness.

The crowd began to slip from their robes, to reveal all manner of men and women, old and young — orange-haired witches of the Cobalt Mountain; forest sorcerers of Ascolais; white-bearded wizards of the Forlorn Land, with babbling small succubi. And one clad in splendid silk was the Prince Datul Omaet of Cansaspara, the city of fallen pylons across the Melantine Gulf. And another creature of scales and staring eyes came of the lizardmen in the barren hills of South Almery. And these two girls, never apart, were Saponids, the near-extinct race from the northern tundras. The slender dark-eyed ones were necrophages from the Land of the Falling Wall. And the dreamy-eyed witch of the blue hair — she dwelt on the Cape of Sad Remembrance and waited at night on the beach for that which came in from the sea.

And as the squat witch with the black ruff and swinging breasts danced, the communicants became exalted, raised their arms, contorted their bodies, pantomimed all the evil and perversion they could set mind to.

Except one — a quiet figure still wrapped in her robe, moving slowly through the saturnalia with a wonderful grace. She stepped up on the dais now, let the robe slip from her body, and Javanne stood revealed in a clinging white gown of mist-stuff, gathered at the waist, fresh and chaste as salt spray. Shining red hair fell over her shoulders like a stream, and curling strands hung over her breasts. Her great gray eyes demure, strawberry mouth a little parted, she gazed back and forth across the crowd. They called and crowed, and Javanne, with tantalizing deliberation, moved her body.

Javanne danced. She raised her arms, wove them down, twisting her body on slender white legs... Javanne danced, her face shining with the most reckless passions. A dim shape dropped from above, a beautiful half-creature, and he joined his body to Javanne's in a fantastic embrace. And the crowd below cried, leapt, rolled, tossed, joined together in a swift culmination of their previous antics.

From the rocks T'sais watched, mind under an intensity no normal brain could understand. But — in strange paradox — the sight and sound fascinated her, reached below the warp, touched the dark chords latent to humanity. Etarr looked down at her, eyes glowing blue fire, and she stared back in a tumult of contradictory emotions. He winced and turned away; at last she looked back to the orgy below — a drug-dream, a heaving of wild flesh in the darting firelight. A palpable aura was cast up, a weft in space meshed of varying depravities. And the demons swooped like birds alighting and joined the delirium. Foul face after face T'sais saw, and each burnt her brain until she thought she must scream and die — visages of leering eye, bulbed cheek, lunatic body, black faces of spiked nose, expressions outraging thought, writhing, hopping, crawling, the spew of the demon-lands. And one had a nose like a three-fold white worm, a mouth that was a putrefying blotch, a mottled jowl and black malformed forehead; the whole a thing of retch and horror. To this Etarr directed T'sais' gaze. She saw and her muscles knotted. "There," said Etarr in a muffled voice, "there is a face twin to the one below this hood." And T'sais, staring at Etarr's black concealment, shrank back.

He chuckled weakly, bitterly... After a moment T'sais reached out and touched his arm. "Etarr."

He turned back to her. "Yes?"

"My brain is flawed. I hate all I see. I cannot control my fears. Nevertheless that which underlies my brain — my blood, my body, my spirit — that which is me loves you, the you underneath the mask."

Etarr studied the white face with a fierce intentness. "How can you love when you hate?"

"I hate you with the hate that I give to all the world; I love you with a feeling nothing else arouses."

Etarr turned away. "We make a strange pair..."

The turmoil, the whimpering joinings of flesh and half-flesh quieted. A tall man in a conical black hat appeared on the dais. He flung back his head, shouted spells to the sky, wove runes in the air with his arms. And as he chanted, high above a gigantic wavering figure began to form, tall, taller than the highest trees, taller than the sky. It shaped slowly, green mists folding and unfolding, and presently the outline was clear — the wavering shape of a woman, beautiful, grave, stately. The figure slowly became steady, glowing with an unearthly green light. She seemed to have golden hair, coiffed in the manner of a dim past, and her clothes were those of the ancients.

The magician who had called her forth screamed, exulted, shouted vast windy taunts that rang past the crags.

"She lives!" murmured T'sais aghast. "She moves! Who is she?"

"It is Ethodea, goddess of mercy, from a time while the sun was still yellow," said Etarr.

The magician flung out his arm and a great bolt of purple fire soared up through the sky and spattered against the dim green form. The calm face twisted in anguish, and the watching demons, witches and necrophages called out in glee. The magician on the dais flung out his arm again and bolt after bolt of purple fire darted up to smite the captive goddess. The whoops and cries of those by the fire were terrible to hear.

Then there came the clear thin call of a bugle, cutting brilliantly through the exultation. The revel jerked breathlessly alert.

The bugle, musical and bright, rang again, louder, a sound alien to the place. And now, breasting over the crags like spume, charged a company of green-clad men, moving with fanatic resolve.

"Valdaran!" cried the magician on the dais, and the green figure of Ethodea wavered and disappeared.

Panic spread through the amphitheater. There were hoarse cries, a milling of lethargic bodies, a cloud of rising shapes as the demons sought flight. A few of the sorcerers stood boldly forth to chant spells of fire, dissolution, and paralysis against the assault, but there was strong counter-magic, and the invaders leapt unscathed into the amphitheater, vaulting the dais. Their swords rose and fell, hacking, slashing, stabbing without mercy or restraint.

"The Green Legion of Valdaran the Just," whispered Etarr. "See, there he stands!" He pointed to a brooding black-clad figure on the crest of the ridge, watching all with a savage satisfaction.

Nor did the demons escape. As they flapped through the night, great birds bestrode by men in green swooped down from the darkness. And these bore tubes which sprayed fans of galling light, and the demons who came within range gave terrible screams and toppled to earth, where they exploded in black dust.

A few sorcerers had escaped to the crags, to dodge and hide among the shadows. T'sais and Etarr heard a scrabbling and panting below. Frantically clambering up the rocks was she whom Etarr had come seeking—Javanne, her red hair streaming back from her clear young face. Etarr made a leap, caught her, clamped her with strong arms.

"Come," he said to T'sais, and bearing the struggling figure, he strode off through the shadows.

At length as they passed down upon the moor, the tumult faded in the distance. Etarr set the woman upon her feet, unclamped her mouth. She caught sight for the first time of him who had seized her. The flame died from her face and through the night a slight smile could be seen. And she combed her long red hair with her fingers, arranging the locks over her shoulders, eyeing Etarr the while. T'sais wandered close, and Javanne turned her a slow appraising glance.

She laughed. "So, Etarr, you have been unfaithful to me; you have found a new lover."

"She is no concern of yours," said Etarr.

"Send her away," said Javanne, "and I will love you again. Remember how you first kissed me beneath the poplars, on the terrace of your villa?"

Etarr gave a short sharp laugh. "There is a single thing I require of you, and that is my face."

And Javanne mocked him. "Your face? What is amiss with the one you wear? You are better suited to it; and in any event, your former face is lost."

"Lost? How so?"

"He who wore it was blasted this night by the Green Legion, may Kraan preserve their living brains in acid!"

Etarr turned his blue eyes off toward the crags.

"So now is your countenance dust, black dust," murmured Javanne. Etarr, in blind rage, stepped forward and struck at the sweetly impudent face. But Javanne took a quick step back.

"Careful, Etarr, lest I mischief you with magic. You may go limping, hopping hence with a body to suit your face. And your beautiful dark-haired child shall be play for demons."

Etarr recovered himself and stood back, eyes smouldering.

"I have magic as well, and even without I would smite you silent with my fist ere you worded the first frame of your spell."

"Ha, that we shall see," cried Javanne, skipping away. "For I have a charm of wonderful brevity." As Etarr lunged at her she spoke a charm. Etarr stopped in mid-stride, his arms fell listless to his side, and he became a creature without volition, all his will drained by the leaching magic.

But Javanne stood in precisely the same posture, and her gray eyes stared dumbly forth. Only T'sais was free — for T'sais wore Pandelume's rune which reflected magic back against him who launched it.

She stood bewildered in the dark night, the two inanimate figures standing like sleep-walkers before her. She ran to Etarr, tugged at his arm. He looked at her with dull eyes.

"Etarr! What is wrong with you?" And Etarr, because his will was paralyzed, forced to answer all questions and obey all orders, replied to her.

"The witch has spoken a spell which leaves me without volition. Therefore I cannot move or speak without command."

"What shall I do? How can I save you?" inquired the distressed girl. And, though Etarr was without volition, he retained his thought and passion. He could give her what information she asked, and nothing more.

"You must order me to a course which will defeat the witch."

"But how will I know this course?"

"You will ask and I will tell you."

"Then would it not be better to order you to act as your brain directs?"

"Yes."

"Then do so; act under all circumstances as Etarr would act."

Thus in the dark of night the spell of Javanne the witch was circumvented and nullified. Etarr was recovered and conducted himself according to his normal promptings. He approached the immobile Javanne.

"Now do you fear me, witch?"

"Yes," said Javanne. "I fear you indeed."

"Is in truth the face you stole from me black dust?"

"Your face is in the black dust of an exploded demon."

The blue eyes looked steadily at her through the slits of the hood.

"How can I recover it?"

"It is mighty magic, a reaching into the past; and now your face is of the past. Magic stronger than mine is required, magic stronger than the wizards of Earth and the demon-worlds possess. I know of two only who are strong enough to make a mold of the past. The one is named Pandelume, who lives in a many-colored land —"

"Embelyon," murmured T'sais.

"— but the spell to journey to this land has been forgotten. Then there is another, who is no wizard, who knows no magic. To get your face, you must seek it of one of these," and Javanne stopped, the question of Etarr answered.

"Who is this latter one?" he asked.

"I know not his name. Far in the past, far beyond thought, so the legend runs, a race of just people lived in a land east of the Maurenron Mountains, past the Land of the Falling Wall, by the shores of a great sea. They built a city of spires and low glass domes, and dwelt in great content. These people had no god, and presently they felt the need of one whom they might worship. So they built a lustrous temple of gold, glass and granite, wide as the Scaum River where it flows through the Valley of Graven Tombs, as long again, and higher than the trees of the north. And this race of honest men assembled in the temple, and all flung a mighty prayer, a worshipful invocation, and, so legend has it, a god molded by the will of this people was brought into being, and he was of their attributes, a divinity of utter justice.

"The city at last crumbled, the temple became shards and splinters, the people vanished. But the god still remains, rooted forever to the place where his people worshipped him. And this god has power beyond magic. To each who faces him, the god wills and justice is done. And let the evil beware, for those who face the god find no whit of mercy. Therefore few dare to bring their faces before this god."

"And to this god we go," said Etarr with grim pleasure. "The three of us, and the three of us shall face justice."

They returned across the moors to Etarr's cabin, and he searched his books for means to transport them to the ancient site. In vain; he had no such magic at his command. He turned to Javanne.

"Do you know of magic to take us to this ancient god?"

"Yes."

"What is this magic?"

"I will call three winged creatures from the Iron Mountains, and they will carry us."

Etarr gazed at Javanne's white face sharply.

"What reward do they demand?"

"They kill those whom they transport."

"Ah, witch," exclaimed Etarr, "even with your will drugged and your answers willy-nilly honest, you contrive to harm us." He stood towering over the beautiful evil of red hair and wet lips. "How may we get to the god unharmed and unmolested?"

"You must put the winged creatures under a charge."

"Summon the things," Etarr ordered, "and place them under the charge; and bind them with all the sorcery you know."

Javanne called the creatures; they settled flapping on great leather wings. She placed them under a pact of safety, and they whined and stamped with disappointment.

And the three mounted, and the creatures took them swiftly through the night air, which already smelled of morning.

East, ever east. Dawn came, and the dim red sun ballooned slowly upward into the dark sky. The black Maurenron Range passed under; and the misty Land of the Falling Wall was left behind. To the south were the deserts of Almery, and an ancient sea-bed filled with jungle; to the north, the wild forests.

All during the day they flew, over dusty waste, dry cliffs, another great range of mountains, and as sunset came they slowly sloped downward over a green parkland.

Ahead shone a glimmering sea. The winged things landed on the wide strand, and Javanne bound them to immobility for their return.

The beach, the woodland behind, both were bare of any trace of the wondrous city of the past. But a half-mile out to sea rose a few broken columns.

"The sea has come," Etarr muttered. "The city has foundered."

He waded out. The sea was calm and shallow. T'sais and Javanne followed. With the water around their waists, and dusk coming from the sky, they came through the broken columns of the ancient temple.

A brooding presence pervaded the place, dispassionate, supernal, of illimitable will and power.

Etarr stood in the center of the old temple.

"God of the past!" he cried. "I know not how you were called, or I would invoke you by name. We three come from a far land to the west to seek justice of you. If you hear and will administer us each our due, give me a sign!"

A low sibilant voice came from the air: "I hear and will give each his due." And each saw a vision of a golden six-armed figure with a round, calm face, sitting impassive in the nave of a monstrous temple.

"I have been bereft of my face," said Etarr. "If you deem me fit, restore me the face I once wore."

The god of the vision extended its six arms.

"I have searched your mind. Justice shall be meted. You may remove your hood." Slowly Etarr doffed his mask. He put his hand to his face. It was his own.

T'sais looked numbly at him. "Etarr!" she gasped. "My brain is whole! — *I see the world*!"

"To each who comes, justice is done," said the sibilant voice.

They heard a moan. They turned and looked at Javanne. Where was the lovely face, the strawberry mouth, the fair skin?

Her nose was a three-fold white squirming thing, her mouth a putrefying blotch. She had dangling mottled jowls and a peaked black forehead. The only thing left of Javanne was the long red hair dangling over her shoulders.

"To each who comes, justice is done," said the voice, and the vision of the temple faded, and once more the cool water of the twilight sea lapped at their waists, and the broken columns leaned black on the sky.

They returned slowly to the winged creatures.

Etarr turned to Javanne. "Go," he commanded. "Fly back to your lair. When the sun sets tomorrow, release yourself from the spell. Never bother us henceforth, for I have magic which will warn me and blast you if you approach."

And Javanne wordlessly bestrode her dark creature and winged off through the night.

Etarr turned to T'sais, and took her hand. He gazed down at her tilted white face, into the eyes glowing with such feverish joy that they seemed afire. He bent and kissed her forehead; then, together, hand in hand, they went to their fretting winged creatures, and so flew back to Ascolais.

IV

Liane the Wayfarer

THROUGH THE DIM FOREST came Liane the Wayfarer, passing along the shadowed glades with a prancing light-footed gait. He whistled, he caroled, he was plainly in high spirits. Around his finger he twirled a bit of wrought bronze — a circlet graved with angular crabbed characters, now stained black.

By excellent chance he had found it, banded around the root of an ancient yew. Hacking it free, he had seen the characters on the inner surface — rude forceful symbols, doubtless the cast of a powerful antique rune... Best take it to a magician and have it tested for sorcery.

Liane made a wry mouth. There were objections to the course. Sometimes it seemed as if all living creatures conspired to exasperate him. Only this morning, the spice merchant — what a tumult he had made dying! How carelessly he had spewed blood on Liane's cock comb sandals! Still, thought Liane, every unpleasantness carried with it compensation. While digging the grave he had found the bronze ring.

And Liane's spirits soared; he laughed in pure joy. He bounded, he leapt. His green cape flapped behind him, the red feather in his cap winked and blinked... But still — Liane slowed his step — he was no whit closer to the mystery of the magic, if magic the ring possessed.

Experiment, that was the word!

He stopped where the ruby sunlight slanted down without hindrance from the high foliage, examined the ring, traced the glyphs with his fingernail. He peered through. A faint film, a flicker? He held it at arm's length. It was clearly a coronet. He whipped off his cap, set the band on his brow, rolled his great golden eyes, preened himself... Odd. It slipped down on his ears. It tipped across his eyes. Darkness. Frantically Liane clawed it off... A bronze ring, a hand's-breadth in diameter. Queer.

He tried again. It slipped down over his head, his shoulders. His head was in the darkness of a strange separate space. Looking down, he saw the level of the outside light dropping as he dropped the ring.

Slowly down... Now it was around his ankles — and in sudden panic, Liane snatched the ring up over his body, emerged blinking into the maroon light of the forest.

He saw a blue-white, green-white flicker against the foliage. It was a Twk-man, mounted on a dragon-fly, and light glinted from the dragon-fly's wings.

Liane called sharply, "Here, sir! Here, sir!"

The Twk-man perched his mount on a twig. "Well, Liane, what do you wish?"

"Watch now, and remember what you see." Liane pulled the ring over his head, dropped it to his feet, lifted it back. He looked up to the Twk-man, who was chewing a leaf. "And what did you see?"

"I saw Liane vanish from mortal sight — except for the red curled toes of his sandals. All else was as air."

"Ha!" cried Liane. "Think of it! Have you ever seen the like?"

The Twk-man asked carelessly, "Do you have salt? I would have salt."

Liane cut his exultations short, eyed the Twk-man closely.

"What news do you bring me?"

"Three erbs killed Florejin the Dream-builder, and burst all his bubbles. The air above the manse was colored for many minutes with the flitting fragments."

"A gram."

"Lord Kandive the Golden has built a barge of carven mo-wood ten lengths high, and it floats on the River Scaum for the Regatta, full of treasure."

"Two grams."

"A golden witch named Lith has come to live on Thamber Meadow. She is quiet and very beautiful."

"Three grams."

"Enough," said the Twk-man, and leaned forward to watch while Liane weighed out the salt in a tiny balance. He packed it in small panniers hanging on each side of the ribbed thorax, then twitched the insect into the air and flicked off through the forest vaults.

Once more Liane tried his bronze ring, and this time brought it entirely past his feet, stepped out of it and brought the ring up into the darkness beside him. What a wonderful sanctuary! A hole whose opening could be hidden inside the hole itself! Down with the ring to his feet, step through, bring it up his slender frame and over his shoulders, out into the forest with a small bronze ring in his hand.

Ho! and off to Thamber Meadow to see the beautiful golden witch.

Her hut was a simple affair of woven reeds — a low dome with two round windows and a low door. He saw Lith at the pond bare-legged among the water shoots, catching frogs for her supper. A white kirtle was gathered up tight around her thighs; stock-still she stood and the dark water rippled rings away from her slender knees.

She was more beautiful than Liane could have imagined, as if one of Florejin's wasted bubbles had burst here on the water. Her skin was pale creamed stirred gold, her hair a denser, wetter gold. Her eyes were like Liane's own, great golden orbs, and hers were wide apart, tilted slightly.

Liane strode forward and planted himself on the bank. She looked up startled, her ripe mouth half-open.

"Behold, golden witch, here is Liane. He has come to welcome you to Thamber; and he offers you his friendship, his love..."

Lith bent, scooped a handful of slime from the bank and flung it into his face.

Shouting the most violent curses, Liane wiped his eyes free, but the door to the hut had slammed shut.

Liane strode to the door and pounded it with his fist.

"Open and show your witch's face, or I burn the hut!"

The door opened, and the girl looked forth, smiling. "What now?"

Liane entered the hut and lunged for the girl, but twenty thin shafts darted out, twenty points pricking his chest. He halted, eyebrows raised, mouth twitching.

"Down, steel," said Lith. The blades snapped from view. "So easily could I seek your vitality," said Lith, "had I willed."

Liane frowned and rubbed his chin as if pondering. "You understand," he said earnestly, "what a witless thing you do. Liane is feared by those who fear fear, loved by those who love love. And you —" his eyes swam the golden glory of her body "— you are ripe as a sweet fruit, you are eager, you glisten and tremble with love. You please Liane, and he will spend much warmness on you."

"No, no," said Lith, with a slow smile. "You are too hasty."

Liane looked at her in surprise. "Indeed?"

"I am Lith," said she. "I am what you say I am. I ferment, I burn, I seethe. Yet I may have no lover but him who has served me. He must be brave, swift, cunning."

"I am he," said Liane. He chewed at his lip. "It is not usually thus. I detest this indecision." He took a step forward. "Come, let us —"

She backed away. "No, no. You forget. How have you served me, how have you gained the right to my love?"

"Absurdity!" stormed Liane. "Look at me! Note my perfect grace, the beauty of my form and feature, my great eyes, as golden as your own, my manifest will and power... It is you who should serve me. That is how I will have it." He sank upon a low divan. "Woman, give me wine."

She shook her head. "In my small domed hut I cannot be forced. Perhaps outside on Thamber Meadow — but in here, among my blue and red tassels, with twenty blades of steel at my call, you must obey me... So choose. Either arise and go, never to return, or else agree to serve me on one small mission, and then have me and all my ardor."

Liane sat straight and stiff. An odd creature, the golden witch. But, indeed, she was worth some exertion, and he would make her pay for her impudence.

"Very well then," he said blandly. "I will serve you. What do you wish? Jewels? I can suffocate you in pearls, blind you with diamonds. I have two emeralds the size of your fist, and they are green oceans, where the gaze is trapped and wanders forever among vertical green prisms..."

"No, no jewels —"

"An enemy, perhaps. Ah, so simple. Liane will kill you ten men. Two steps forward, thrust — *thus*!" He lunged. "And souls go thrilling up like bubbles in a beaker of mead."

"No. I want no killing."

He sat back, frowning. "What then?"

She stepped to the back of the room and pulled at a drape. It swung aside, displaying a golden tapestry. The scene was a valley bounded by two steep mountains, a broad valley where a placid river ran, past a quiet village and so into a grove of trees. Golden was the river, golden the mountains, golden the trees — golds so various, so rich, so subtle that the effect was like a many-colored landscape. But the tapestry had been rudely hacked in half.

Liane was entranced. "Exquisite, exquisite ..."

Lith said, "It is the Magic Valley of Ariventa so depicted. The other half has been stolen from me, and its recovery is the service I wish of you."

"Where is the other half?" demanded Liane. "Who is the dastard?"

Now she watched him closely. "Have you ever heard of Chun? Chun the Unavoidable?"

Liane considered. "No."

"He stole the half to my tapestry, and hung it in a marble hall, and this hall is in the ruins to the north of Kaiin."

"Ha!" muttered Liane.

"The hall is by the Place of Whispers, and is marked by a leaning column with a black medallion of a phoenix and a two-headed lizard."

"I go," said Liane. He rose. "One day to Kaiin, one day to steal, one day to return. Three days."

Lith followed him to the door. "Beware of Chun the Unavoidable," she whispered.

And Liane strode away whistling, the red feather bobbing in his green cap. Lith watched him, then turned and slowly approached the golden tapestry. "Golden Ariventa," she whispered, "my heart cries and hurts with longing for you ..."

The Derna is a swifter, thinner river than the Scaum, its bosomy sister to the south. And where the Scaum wallows through a broad dale, purple with horse-blossom, pocked white and gray with crumbling castles, the Derna has sheered a steep canyon, overhung by forested bluffs.

An ancient flint road long ago followed the course of the Derna, but now the exaggeration of the meandering has cut into the pavement, so that Liane, treading the road to Kaiin, was occasionally forced to leave the road and make a detour through banks of thorn and tubegrass which whistled in the breeze.

The red sun, drifting across the universe like an old man creeping to his death-bed, hung low to the horizon when Liane breasted Porphiron Scar, looked across white-walled Kaiin and the blue bay of Sanreale beyond.

Directly below was the market-place, a medley of stalls selling fruit, slabs of pale meat, molluscs from the slime banks, dull flagons of wine. And the quiet people of Kaiin moved among the stalls, buying their sustenance, carrying it loosely to their stone chambers.

Beyond the market-place rose a bank of ruined columns, like broken teeth — legs to the arena built two hundred feet from the ground by Mad King Shin; beyond, in a grove of bay trees, the glossy dome of the palace was visible, where Kandive the Golden ruled Kaiin and as much of Ascolais as one could see from a vantage on Porphiron Scar.

The Derna, no longer a flow of clear water, poured through a network of dank canals and subterranean tubes, and finally seeped past rotting wharves into the Bay of Sanreale.

A bed for the night, thought Liane; then to his business in the morning.

He leapt down the zig-zag steps — back, forth, back, forth — and came out into the market-place. And now he put on a grave demeanor. Liane the Wayfarer was not unknown in Kaiin, and many were ill-minded enough to work him harm.

He moved sedately in the shade of the Pannone Wall, turned through a narrow cobbled street, bordered by old wooden houses glowing the rich brown of old stump-water in the rays of the setting sun, and so came to a small square and the high stone face of the Magician's Inn.

The host, a small fat man, sad of eye, with a small fat nose the identical shape of his body, was scraping ashes from the hearth. He straightened his back and hurried behind the counter of his little alcove.

Liane said, "A chamber, well-aired, and a supper of mushrooms, wine and oysters."

The innkeeper bowed humbly.

"Indeed, sir — and how will you pay?"

Liane flung down a leather sack, taken this very morning. The innkeeper raised his eyebrows in pleasure at the fragrance.

"The ground buds of the spase-bush, brought from a far land," said Liane.

"Excellent, excellent... Your chamber sir, and your supper at once."

As Liane ate, several other guests of the house appeared and sat before the fire with wine, and the talk grew large, and dwelt on wizards of the past and the great days of magic.

"Great Phandaal knew a lore now forgot," said one old man with hair dyed orange. "He tied white and black strings to the legs of sparrows and sent them veering to his direction. And where they wove their magic woof, great trees appeared, laden with flowers, fruits, nuts, or bulbs of rare liqueurs. It is said that thus he wove Great Da Forest on the shores of Sanra Water."

"Ha," said a dour man in a garment of dark blue, brown and black, "this I can do." He brought forth a bit of string, flicked it, whirled it, spoke a quiet word, and the vitality of the pattern fused the string into a tongue of red and yellow fire, which danced, curled, darted back and forth along the table till the dour man killed it with a gesture.

"And this I can do," said a hooded figure in a black cape sprinkled with silver circles. He brought forth a small tray, laid it on the table and sprinkled therein a pinch of ashes from the hearth. He brought forth a whistle and blew a clear tone, and up from the tray came glittering motes, flashing the prismatic colors red, blue, green, yellow. They floated up a foot and burst in coruscations of brilliant colors, each a beautiful star-shaped pattern, and each burst sounded a tiny repetition of the original tone — the clearest, purest sound in the world. The motes became fewer, the magician blew a different tone, and again the motes floated up to burst in glorious ornamental spangles. Another time — another swarm of motes. At last the magician replaced his whistle, wiped off the tray, tucked it inside his cloak and lapsed back to silence.

Now the other wizards surged forward, and soon the air above the table swarmed with visions, quivered with spells. One showed the group nine new colors of ineffable charm and radiance; another caused a mouth to form on the landlord's forehead and revile the crowd, much to the landlord's discomfiture, since it was his own voice. Another displayed a green glass bottle from which the face of a demon peered and grimaced; another a ball of pure crystal which rolled back and forward to the command of the sorcerer who owned it, and who claimed it to be an earring of the fabled master Sankaferrin.

Liane had attentively watched all, crowing in delight at the bottled imp, and trying to cozen the obedient crystal from its owner, without success.

And Liane became pettish, complaining that the world was full of rock-hearted men, but the sorcerer with the crystal earring remained indifferent, and even when Liane spread out twelve packets of rare spice he refused to part with his toy.

Liane pleaded, "I wish only to please the witch Lith."

"Please her with the spice, then."

Liane said ingenuously, "Indeed, she has but one wish, a bit of tapestry which I must steal from Chun the Unavoidable."

And he looked from face to suddenly silent face.

"What causes such immediate sobriety? Ho, Landlord, more wine!"

The sorcerer with the earring said, "If the floor swam ankle-deep with wine — the rich red wine of Tanvilkat — the leaden print of that name would still ride the air."

"Ha," laughed Liane, "let only a taste of that wine pass your lips, and the fumes would erase all memory."

"See his eyes," came a whisper. "Great and golden."

"And quick to see," spoke Liane. "And these legs — quick to run, fleet as starlight on the waves. And this arm — quick to stab with steel. And my magic — which will set me to a refuge that is out of all cognizance." He gulped wine from a beaker. "Now behold. This is magic from antique days." He set the bronze band over his head, stepped through, brought it up inside the darkness. When he deemed that sufficient time had elapsed, he stepped through once more.

The fire glowed, the landlord stood in his alcove, Liane's wine was at hand. But of the assembled magicians, there was no trace.

Liane looked about in puzzlement. "And where are my wizardly friends?"

The landlord turned his head. “They took to their chambers; the name you spoke weighed on their souls.”

And Liane drank his wine in frowning silence.

Next morning he left the inn and picked a roundabout way to the Old Town — a gray wilderness of tumbled pillars, weathered blocks of sandstone, slumped pediments with crumbled inscriptions, flagged terraces overgrown with rusty moss. Lizards, snakes, insects crawled the ruins; no other life did he see.

Threading a way through the rubble, he almost stumbled on a corpse — the body of a youth, one who stared at the sky with empty eye-sockets.

Liane felt a presence. He leapt back, rapier half-bared. A stooped old man stood watching him. He spoke in a feeble, quavering voice: “And what will you have in the Old Town?”

Liane replaced his rapier. “I seek the Place of Whispers. Perhaps you will direct me.”

The old man made a croaking sound at the back of his throat. “Another? Another? When will it cease…” He motioned to the corpse. “This one came yesterday seeking the Place of Whispers. He would steal from Chun the Unavoidable. See him now.” He turned away. “Come with me.” He disappeared over a tumble of rock.

Liane followed. The old man stood by another corpse with eye-sockets bereft and bloody. “This one came four days ago, and he met Chun the Unavoidable… And over there behind the arch is another still, a great warrior in cloison armor. And there — and there —” he pointed, pointed. “And there — and there — like crushed flies.”

He turned his watery blue gaze back to Liane. “Return, young man, return — lest your body lie here in its green cloak to rot on the flagstones.”

Liane drew his rapier and flourished it. “I am Liane the Wayfarer; let them who offend me have fear. And where is the Place of Whispers?”

“If you must know,” said the old man, “it is beyond that broken obelisk. But you go to your peril.”

“I am Liane the Wayfarer. Peril goes with me.”

The old man stood like a piece of weathered statuary as Liane strode off.

And Liane asked himself, suppose this old man were an agent of Chun, and at this minute were on his way to warn him?...Best to take all precautions. He leapt up on a high entablature and ran crouching back to where he had left the ancient.

Here he came, muttering to himself, leaning on his staff. Liane dropped a block of granite as large as his head. A thud, a croak, a gasp — and Liane went his way.

He strode past the broken obelisk into a wide court — the Place of Whispers. Directly opposite was a long wide hall, marked by a leaning column with a big black medallion, the sign of a phoenix and a two-headed lizard.

Liane merged himself with the shadow of a wall, and stood watching like a wolf, alert for any flicker of motion.

All was quiet. The sunlight invested the ruins with dreary splendor. To all sides, as far as the eye could reach, was broken stone, a wasteland leached by a thousand rains, until now the sense of man had departed and the stone was one with the natural earth.

The sun moved across the dark-blue sky. Liane presently stole from his vantage-point and circled the hall. No sight nor sign did he see.

He approached the building from the rear and pressed his ear to the stone. It was dead, without vibration. Around the side — watching up, down, to all sides; a breach in the wall. Liane peered inside. At the back hung half a golden tapestry. Otherwise the hall was empty.

Liane looked up, down, this side, that. There was nothing in sight. He continued around the hall.

He came to another broken place. He looked within. To the rear hung the golden tapestry. Nothing else, to right or left, no sight or sound.

Liane continued to the front of the hall and sought into the eaves; dead as dust.

He had a clear view of the room. Bare, barren, except for the bit of golden tapestry.

Liane entered, striding with long soft steps. He halted in the middle of the floor. Light came to him from all sides except the rear wall. There were a dozen openings from which to flee and no sound except the dull thudding of his heart.

He took two steps forward. The tapestry was almost at his fingertips.

He stepped forward and swiftly jerked the tapestry down from the wall.

And behind was Chun the Unavoidable.

Liane screamed. He turned on paralyzed legs and they were leaden, like legs in a dream which refused to run.

Chun dropped out of the wall and advanced. Over his shiny black back he wore a robe of eyeballs threaded on silk.

Liane was running, fleetly now. He sprang, he soared. The tips of his toes scarcely touched the ground. Out the hall, across the square, into the wilderness of broken statues and fallen columns. And behind came Chun, running like a dog.

Liane sped along the crest of a wall and sprang a great gap to a shattered fountain. Behind came Chun.

Liane darted up a narrow alley, climbed over a pile of refuse, over a roof, down into a court. Behind came Chun.

Liane sped down a wide avenue lined with a few stunted old cypress trees, and he heard Chun close at his heels. He turned into an archway, pulled his bronze ring over his head, down to his feet. He stepped through, brought the ring up inside the darkness. Sanctuary. He was alone in a dark magic space, vanished from earthly gaze and knowledge. Brooding silence, dead space…

He felt a stir behind him, a breath of air. At his elbow a voice said, "I am Chun the Unavoidable."

Lith sat on her couch near the candles, weaving a cap from frogskins. The door to her hut was barred, the windows shuttered. Outside, Thamber Meadow dwelled in darkness.

A scrape at her door, a creak as the lock was tested. Lith became rigid and stared at the door.

A voice said, "Tonight, O Lith, tonight it is two long bright threads for you. Two because the eyes were so great, so large, so golden…"

Lith sat quiet. She waited an hour; then, creeping to the door, she listened. The sense of presence was absent. A frog croaked nearby.

She eased the door ajar, found the threads and closed the door. She ran to her golden tapestry and fitted the threads into the ravelled warp.

And she stared at the golden valley, sick with longing for Ariventa, and tears blurred out the peaceful river, the quiet golden forest. "The cloth slowly grows wider...One day it will be done, and I will come home..."

V

Ulan Dhor Ends a Dream

Prince Kandive the Golden spoke earnestly to his nephew Ulan Dhor. "It must be understood that the expansion of craft and the new lore will be shared between us."

Ulan Dhor, a slender young man, pale of skin, with the blackest of hair, eyes, and eyebrows, smiled ruefully. "But it is I who journey the forgotten water, I who must beat down the sea-demons with my oar."

Kandive leaned back into his cushions and tapped his nose with a ferrule of carved jade.

"And it is I who make the venture possible. Further, I am already an accomplished wizard; the increment of lore will merely enhance my craft. You, not even a novice, will gain such knowledge as to rank you among the magicians of Ascolais. This is a far cry from your present ineffectual status. Seen in this light, my gain is small, yours is great."

Ulan Dhor grimaced. "True enough, though I dispute the word 'ineffectual'. I know Phandaal's Critique of the Chill, I am reckoned a master of the sword, ranked among the Eight Delaphasians as a..."

"Pah!" sneered Kandive. "The vapid mannerisms of pale people, using up their lives. Mincing murder, extravagant debauchery, while Earth passes its last hours, and none of you have ventured a mile from Kaiin."

Ulan Dhor held his tongue, reflecting that Prince Kandive the Golden was not known to scorn the pleasures of wine, couch, or table; and that his farthest known sally from the domed palace had taken him to his carven barge on the River Scaum.

Kandive, appeased by Ulan Dhor's silence, brought forward an ivory box. "Thus and so. If we are agreed, I will invest you with knowledge."

Ulan Dhor nodded. "We are agreed."

Kandive said, "The mission will take you to the lost city Ampridatvir." He watched Ulan Dhor's face from sidelong eyes; Ulan Dhor maintained an even expression.

"I have never seen it," continued Kandive. "Porrina the Ninth lists it as the last of the Olek'hnit cities, situated on an island in the North Melantine." He opened the box. "This tale I found in an ancient bundle of scrolls — the testament of a poet who fled Ampridatvir after the death of Rogol Domedonfors, their last great leader, a magician of great force, mentioned forty-three times in the Cyclopedia ..."

Kandive brought forth a crackling scroll, and, whipping it open, read:

> *Ampridatvir now is lost. My people have forsaken the doctrine of strength and discipline and concern themselves only with superstition and theology. Unending is the bicker: Is Pansiu the excellent principle and Cazdal depraved, or is Cazdal the virtuous god, and Pansiu the essential evil?*
>
> *These questions are debated with fire and steel, and the memory sickens me; now I leave Ampridatvir to the decline which must surely come, and remove to the kind valley of Mel-Palusas, where I will end this firefly life of mine.*
>
> *I have known the Ampridatvir of old; I have seen the towers glowing with marvellous light, thrusting beams through the night to challenge the sun itself. Then Ampridatvir was beautiful — ah! My heart pains when I think of the olden city. Semir vines cascaded from a thousand hanging gardens, water ran blue as vaul-stone in the three canals. Metal cars rolled the streets, metal hulls swarmed the air as thick as bees around a hive — for marvel of marvels, we had devised wefts of spitting fire to spurn the weighty power of Earth ... But even in my life I saw the leaching of spirit. A surfeit of honey cloys the tongue; a surfeit of wine addles the brain; so a surfeit of ease guts a man of strength. Light, warmth, food, water, were free to all men, and gained by a minimum of effort. So the*

people of Ampridatvir, released from toil, gave increasing attention to faddishness, perversity, and the occult.

To the furthest reach of my memory, Rogol Domedonfors ruled the city. He knew lore of all ages, secrets of fire and light, gravity and counter-gravity, the knowledge of superphysic numeration, metathasm, corolopsis. In spite of his profundity, he was impractical in his rule, and blind to the softening of Ampridatvirian spirit. Such weakness and lethargy as he saw he ascribed to a lack of education, and in his last years he evolved a tremendous machine to release men from all labor, and thus permit full leisure for meditation and ascetic discipline.

While Rogol Domedonfors completed his great work, the city dissolved into turbulence — the result of a freak religious hysteria.

The rival sects of Pansiu and Cazdal had long existed, but few other than the priests heeded the dispute. Suddenly the cults became fashionable; the population flocked to worship one or the other of the deities. The priests, long-jealous rivals, were delighted with their new power, and exhorted the converts to a crusading zeal. Friction arose, emotion waxed, there was rioting and violence. And on one evil day a stone struck Rogol Domedonfors, toppled him from a balcony.

Crippled and wasting but refusing to die, Rogol Domedonfors completed his underground mechanism, installed vestibules throughout the city, and then took to his death-bed. He issued one directive to his new machine, and when Ampridatvir awoke the next morning, the people found their city without power or light, the food factories quiet, the canals diverted.

In terror they rushed to Rogol Domedonfors, who said: "I have long been blind to your decadence and eccentricities; now I despise you; you have been the death of me."

"But the city dies! The race perishes!" they cried.

"You must save yourselves," Rogol Domedonfors told them. "You have ignored the ancient wisdom, you have been too indolent to learn, you have sought easy complacence from religion, rather than facing manfully to the world. I have resolved to impose a bitter experience upon you, which I hope will be salutary."

He called the rival priests of Pansiu and Cazdal, and handed to each a tablet of transparent metal.

"These tablets singly are useless; laid together a message may be read. He who reads the message will have the key to the ancient knowledge, and will wield the power I had planned for my own use. Now go, and I will die."

The priests, glaring at each other, departed, called their followers, and so began a great war.

The body of Rogol Domedonfors was never found, and some say his skeleton still lies in the passages below the city. The tablets are housed in the rival temples. By night there is murder, by day there is starvation in the streets. Many have fled to the mainland, and now I follow, leaving Ampridatvir, the last home of the race. I will build a wooden hut on the slope of Mount Liu and live out my days in the valley of Mel-Palusas.

Kandive twisted the scroll and replaced it in the box. "Your task," he told Ulan Dhor, "is to journey to Ampridatvir and recover the magic of Rogol Domedonfors."

Ulan Dhor said thoughtfully, "It was a long time ago... Thousands of years..."

"Correct," said Kandive. "However, none of the histories or indices make further mention of Rogol Domedonfors, and therefore I believe that the wisdom of Rogol Domedonfors still remains to be found in ancient Ampridatvir."

Three weeks Ulan Dhor sailed the nerveless ocean. The sun rose bright as blood from the horizon and belled across the sky, and the water was calm, save for the ruffle of the breeze and the twin widening marks of Ulan Dhor's wake.

Then came the setting, the last sad glance across the world; then purple twilight and the night. The old stars spanned the sky and the wake behind Ulan Dhor shone ghastly white. Then did he watch for heavings of the surface, for he felt greatly alone on the dark face of the ocean.

Three weeks Ulan Dhor sailed the Melantine Gulf, to the north and west, and one morning he saw to the right the dark shadow of coastland and to the left the loom of an island, almost lost in the haze.

Close off his bow floated an ungainly barge, moving sluggishly under a square sail of plaited reeds.

Ulan Dhor laid a course so as to draw alongside, and saw on the barge two men in coarse green smocks trolling for fish. They had oat-yellow hair and blue eyes, and they wore expressions of stupefaction.

Ulan Dhor dropped his sail and laid hold of the barge. The fishermen neither moved nor spoke.

Ulan Dhor said, "You seem unfamiliar with the sight of man."

The older man broke into a nervous chant which Ulan Dhor understood to be an invocation against demons and frits.

Ulan Dhor laughed. "Why do you inveigh against me? I am a man like yourself."

The younger man said in a broad dialect: "We reason you to be a demon. First, there are none of our race with night-black hair and eyes. Second, the Word of Pansiu denies the existence of all other men. Therefore you can be no man, and must be a demon."

The older man said under his hand, "Hold your tongue; speak no word. He will curse the tones of your voice..."

"You are wrong, I assure you," replied Ulan Dhor politely. "Have either of you ever seen a demon?"

"None but the Gauns."

"Do I resemble the Gauns?"

"Not at all," admitted the older man. His companion indicated Ulan Dhor's dull scarlet coat and green trousers. "He is evidently a Raider; note the color of his garb."

Ulan Dhor said, "No, I am neither Raider nor demon. I am merely a man..."

"No men exist except the Greens — so says Pansiu."

Ulan Dhor threw back his head and laughed. "Earth is but wilderness and ruins, true enough, but many men yet walk abroad... Tell me, is the city Ampridatvir to be found on that island ahead?"

The younger man nodded.

"And you live there?"

Again the young man assented.

Ulan Dhor said uncomfortably, "I understood that Ampridatvir was a deserted ruin — forlorn, desolate."

The young man asked with a shrewd expression, "And what do you seek at Ampridatvir?"

Ulan Dhor thought, I will mention the tablets and observe their reaction. It is well to learn if these tablets are known, and if so, how they are regarded. He said, "I have sailed three weeks to find Ampridatvir and investigate some legendary tablets..."

"Ah," said the older man. "The tablets! He is a Raider, then. I see it clearly. Note his green trousers. A Raider for the Greens..."

Ulan Dhor, expecting hostility as a result of this identification, was surprised to find a more pleasant expression on the faces of the men, as if now they had resolved a troublesome paradox. Very well, he thought, if that is how they will have it, let it be.

The younger man wished total clarity. "Is that your claim then, dark man? Do you wear red as a Raider for the Greens?"

Ulan Dhor said cautiously, "My plans are not settled."

"But you wear red! That is the color the Raiders wear!"

Here is a peculiarly disrupted way of thinking, reflected Ulan Dhor. It is almost as if a rock blocked the stream of their thought and diverted the current in a splash and a spray. He said, "Where I come from, a man wears such colors as he chooses."

The older man said eagerly, "But you wear Green, so evidently you have chosen to raid for the Greens."

Ulan Dhor shrugged, sensing the block across a mental channel. "If you wish... What others are there?"

"None, no other," replied the older man. "We are the Greens of Ampridatvir."

"Then — whom does a Raider raid?"

The younger man moved uneasily and pulled in his line. "He raids a ruined temple to the demon Cazdal, for the lost tablet of Rogol Domedonfors."

"In that case," said Ulan Dhor, "I might become a Raider."

"For the Greens," said the old man, peering at him sidewise.

"Enough, enough," said the other. "The sun is past the zenith. We had best be homeward."

"Aye, aye," said the older man, with sudden energy. "The sun drops."

The younger man looked at Ulan Dhor. "If you propose to raid, you had best come with us."

Ulan Dhor passed a line to the barge, adding his fabric sail to the plaited reeds, and they turned their bows toward shore.

It was very beautiful, crossing the sunny afternoon swells toward the forested island, and as they rounded the eastern cape, Ampridatvir came into view.

A line of low buildings faced the harbor, and beyond rose such towers as Ulan Dhor had never imagined to exist — metal spires soaring past the central height of the island to glisten in the light of the setting sun. Such cities were legends of the past, dreams of the time when the Earth was young.

Ulan Dhor stared speculatively at the barge, at the coarse green cloaks of the fishermen. Were they peasants? Would he become a butt for ridicule, thus arriving at the glistening city? He turned uncomfortably back to the island, chewing his lips. According to Kandive, Ampridatvir would be toppled columns and rubble, like the Old Town above Kaiin…

The sun dropped against the water, and now Ulan Dhor, with a sudden shock, noticed the crumble at the base of the towers; here was his expectation, as much desolation as Kandive had predicted. Strangely the fact gave Ampridatvir an added majesty, the dignity of a lost monument.

The wind had slackened, the progress of boat and barge was slow indeed. The fishermen betrayed anxiety, muttering to each other, adjusting their sail to draw its best, tightening their stays. But before they drifted inside the breakwater, purple twilight had dropped across the city, and the towers became tremendous black monoliths. In near-darkness they tied to a landing of logs, among other barges, some painted green, others gray.

Ulan Dhor jumped up to the dock. "A moment," said the younger fisherman, eyeing Ulan Dhor's red coat. "It would be unwise to dress thus, even at night." He rummaged through a box and brought forth a green cape, ragged and smelling of fish. "Wear this, and hold the hood over your black hair…"

Ulan Dhor obeyed with a private grimace of distaste. He asked, "Where may I sup and bed tonight? Are there inns or hostels in Ampridatvir?"

The younger man said without enthusiasm, "You may pass the night at my hall."

The fishermen slung the day's catch over their shoulders, climbed to the dock, and peered anxiously through the rubble.

"You are ill at ease," observed Ulan Dhor.

"Aye," said the younger man. "At night the Gauns roam the streets."

"What are the Gauns?"

"Demons."

"There are many varieties of demons," Ulan Dhor said lightly. "What be these?"

"They are like horrible men. They have great long arms that clutch and rend..."

"Ho!" muttered Ulan Dhor, feeling for his sword hilt. "Why do you permit them abroad?"

"We cannot harm them. They are fierce and strong — but fortunately not too agile. With luck and watchfulness..."

Ulan Dhor now searched the rubble with an expression as careful as the fishermen's. These people were familiar with the dangers of the place; he would obey their counsel until he knew better.

They threaded the first tumble of ruins, entered a canyon shadowed from the afterglow by the pinnacles to either side, brimming with gloom.

Deadness! thought Ulan Dhor. The place was under the pall of dusty death. Where were the active millions of long ago Ampridatvir? Dead dust, their moisture mingled in the ocean, beside that of every other man and woman who had lived on Earth.

Ulan Dhor and the two fishermen moved down the avenue, pygmy figures wandering a dream-city, and Ulan Dhor looked coldly from side to side... Prince Kandive had spoken the truth. Ampridatvir was the very definition of antiquity. The windows gaped black, concrete had cracked, balconies hung crazily, terraces were mounded with dust, debris filled the street — blocks of stone from fallen columns, crushed and battered metal.

But Ampridatvir still moved with a weird unending life where the builders had used ageless substance, eternal energies. Strips of a dark glistening material flowed like water at each side of the street — slowly at the edges, rapidly at the center.

The fishermen matter-of-factly stepped on this strip, and Ulan Dhor gingerly followed them to the swift center. "I see roads flowing like rivers in Ampridatvir," he said. "You call me demon; truly I think the glove is on the other hand."

"It is no magic," said the younger man shortly. "It is the way of Ampridatvir."

At regular intervals along the street stood stone vestibules about ten feet high that had the appearance of sheltering ramps leading below the street.

"What lies below?" inquired Ulan Dhor.

The fishermen shrugged. "The doors are tight. No man has ever gone through. Legend says it was the last work of Rogol Domedonfors."

Ulan Dhor withheld further questions, observing a growing nervousness in the fishermen. Infected by their apprehension he kept his hand at his sword.

"None live in this part of Ampridatvir," said the old fisherman in a hoarse whisper. "It is ancient beyond imagining, ridden with ghosts."

The streets broke into a central square, the towers fell away before them. The sliding strip coasted to a stop, like water flowing into a pool. Here glowed the first artificial light Ulan Dhor had seen — a bright globe hung on a looping metal stanchion.

In this light Ulan Dhor saw a youth in a gray cloak hurrying across the square… A movement among the ruins; the fishermen gasped, crouched. A corpse-pale creature sprang out into the light. Its arms hung knotted and long; dirty fur covered its legs. Great eyes glared from a peaked, fungus-white skull; two fangs hung over the undershot mouth. It leapt upon the wretch in the gray robe and tucked him under his arm; then, turning, gave Ulan Dhor and the fishermen a look of baleful triumph. And now they saw that the victim was a woman…

Ulan Dhor drew his sword. "No, no!" whispered the older man. "The Gaun will go its way!"

"But the woman it has taken! We can save her!"

"The Gaun has seized no one." The old man clutched at his shoulder.

"Are you blind, man?" cried Ulan Dhor.

"There are none in Ampridatvir but the Greens," said the younger man. "Stay by us."

Ulan Dhor hesitated. Was the woman in gray, then, a ghost? If so, why did not the fishermen say as much?...The Gaun, with insolent leisure, stalked toward a long edifice of dark tumbled arches.

Ulan Dhor ran across the white square of ancient Ampridatvir.

The monster twisted to face him and flung out a great knotted arm, as long as a man was tall, ending in a white-furred clump of fingers. Ulan Dhor hewed a tremendous blow with his sword; the Gaun's forearm dangled by a shred of flesh and bone-splinter.

Jumping back to avoid the spray of blood, Ulan Dhor ducked the grasp of the other arm as it swung past. He hacked again, another great blow, and the second forearm dangled loosely. He sprang close, plunged his blade at the creature's eye and struck up into the beast's skull-case.

The creature died in a series of wild capers, maniac throes that took it dancing around the square.

Ulan Dhor, panting, fighting nausea, looked down to the wide-eyed woman. She was rising weakly to her feet. He reached an arm to steady her, noticing that she was slim and young, with blonde hair hanging loosely to the level of her jaw. She had a pleasant, pretty face, thought Ulan Dhor — candid, clear-eyed, innocent.

She appeared not to notice him, but stood half-turned away, wrapping herself in her gray cloak. Ulan Dhor began to fear that the shock had affected her mind. He moved forward and peered into her face.

"Are you well? Did the beast harm you?"

Surprise came over her face, almost as if Ulan Dhor were another Gaun. Her gaze brushed his green cloak, quickly moved back to his face, his black hair.

"Who...are you?" she whispered.

"A stranger," said Ulan Dhor, "and much puzzled by the ways of Ampridatvir." He looked around for the fishermen; they were nowhere in sight.

"A stranger?" the girl asked. "But Cazdal's Tract tells us that the Gauns have destroyed all men but the Grays of Ampridatvir."

"Cazdal is as incorrect as Pansiu," remarked Ulan Dhor. "There are still many men in the world."

"I must believe," said the girl. "You speak, you exist — so much is clear."

Ulan Dhor noticed that she kept her eyes averted from the green cloak. It stank of fish; without further ado he cast it aside.

Her glance went to his red coat. "A Raider…"

"No, no, no!" exclaimed Ulan Dhor. "In truth, I find this talk of color tiresome. I am Ulan Dhor of Kaiin, nephew to Prince Kandive the Golden, and my mission is to seek the tablets of Rogol Domedonfors."

The girl smiled wanly. "Thus do the Raiders, and thus they dress in red, and then every man's hand is turned against them, for when they are in red, who knows whether they be Grays or…"

"Or what?"

She appeared confused, as if this facet to the question had not occurred to her. "Ghosts? Demons? There are strange manifestations in Ampridatvir."

"Beyond argument," agreed Ulan Dhor. He glanced across the square. "If you wish, I will guard you to your home; and perhaps there will be a corner where I may sleep tonight."

She said, "I owe you my life, and I will help you as best I can. But I dare not take you to my hall." Her eyes drifted down his body as far as his green trousers and veered away. "There would be confusion and unending explanations…"

Ulan Dhor said obliquely, "You have a mate, then?"

She glanced at him swiftly — a strange coquetry, strange flirtation there in the shadows of ancient Ampridatvir, the girl in the coarse gray cloak, her head tilted sideways and the yellow hair falling clear to her shoulder; Ulan Dhor elegant, darkly aquiline, in full command of his soul.

"No," she said. "There have been none, so far." A slight sound disturbed her; she jerked, looked fearfully across the square.

"There may be more Gauns. I can take you to a safe place; then tomorrow we will talk…"

She led him through an arched portico into one of the towers, up to a mezzanine floor. "You'll be safe here till morning." She squeezed his arm. "I'll bring you food, if you'll wait for me…"

"I'll wait."

Her gaze fell with the strange half-averted wavering of the eyes to his red coat, just brushed his green trousers. "And I'll bring you a cloak." She departed. Ulan Dhor saw her flit down the stair and out of the tower like a wraith. She was gone.

He settled himself on the floor. It was a soft elastic substance, warm to touch... A strange city, thought Ulan Dhor, a strange people, reacting to unguessed compulsions. Or were they ghosts, in truth?

He fell into a series of spasmodic dozes, and awoke at last to find the wan pink of the latter-day dawn seeping through the arched portico.

He rose to his feet, rubbed his face, and, after a moment's hesitation, descended from the mezzanine to the floor of the tower and walked out into the street. A child in a gray smock saw his red coat, flicked his eyes away from the green trousers, screamed in terror, and ran across the square.

Ulan Dhor retreated into the shadows with a curse. He had expected desolation. Hostility he could have countered or fled, but this bewildered fright left him helpless.

A shape appeared at the entrance—the girl. She peered through the shadows; her face was drawn, anxious. Ulan Dhor appeared. She smiled suddenly and her face changed.

"I brought your breakfast," she said, "also a decent garment."

She lay bread and smoked fish before him, and poured warm herb tea from an earthenware jar.

As he ate he watched her, and she watched him. There was a tension in their relations; she felt incompletely secure, and he could sense the pressures on her mind.

"What is your name?" she asked.

"I am Ulan Dhor. And you?"

"Elai."

"Elai... Is that all?"

"Do I need more? It is sufficient, is it not?"

"Oh, indeed."

She seated herself cross-legged before him.

"Tell me about the land from which you come."

Ulan Dhor said, "Ascolais now is mostly a great forest, where few care to venture. I live in Kaiin, a very old city, perhaps as old as Ampridatvir, but we have no such towers and floating roads. We live in the old time palaces of marble and wood, even the poorest and most menial. Indeed, some beautiful manses fall to ruins for lack of tenants."

"And what is your color?" she asked in a tentative voice.

Ulan Dhor said impatiently, "Such nonsense. We wear all colors; no one thinks one way or the other about it...Why do you worry about color so? For instance, why do you wear gray and not green?"

Her gaze wavered and broke from his; she clenched her hands restlessly. "Green? That is the color of the demon Pansiu. No one in Ampridatvir wears green."

"Certainly people wear green," said Ulan Dhor. "I met two fishermen yesterday at sea wearing green, and they guided me into the city."

She shook her head, smiling sadly. "You are mistaken."

Ulan Dhor sat back. He said presently, "A child saw me this morning and ran off screaming."

"Because of your red cloak," said Elai. "When a man wishes to win honor for himself, he dons a red coat and sets forth across the city to the ancient deserted temple of Pansiu, to seek the lost half of Rogol Domedonfors' tablet. Legend says that when the Grays recover the lost tablet, then will their power be strong once more."

"If the temple is deserted," asked Ulan Dhor dryly, "why has not some man taken the tablet?"

She shrugged and looked vaguely into space. "We believe that it is guarded by ghosts...At any rate, sometimes a man in red is found raiding Cazdal's temple also, whereupon he is killed. A man in red is therefore everybody's enemy, and every hand is turned against him."

Ulan Dhor rose to his feet and wrapped himself in the gray robe the girl had brought.

"What are your plans?" she asked, rising quickly.

"I wish to look upon the tablets of Rogol Domedonfors, both in Cazdal's Temple and in Pansiu's."

She shook her head. "Impossible. Cazdal's Temple is forbidden to all but the venerable priests, and Pansiu's Temple is guarded by ghosts."

Ulan Dhor grinned. "If you'll show me where the temples are situated..."

She said, "I'll go with you...But you must remain wrapped in the cloak, or it will go badly for both of us."

They stepped out into the sunlight. The square was dotted with slow-moving groups of men and women. Some wore green, others wore gray, and Ulan Dhor saw that there was no intercourse between the two. Greens paused by little green-painted booths selling fish, leather, fruit, meal, pottery, baskets. Grays bought from identical shops which were painted gray. He saw two groups of children, one in green rags, the other in gray, playing ten feet apart, acknowledging each other by not so much as a glance. A ball of tied rags rolled from the Gray children into the scuffling group of Greens. A Gray child ran over, picked up the ball from under the feet of a Green child, and neither took the slightest notice of the other.

"Strange," muttered Ulan Dhor. "Strange."

"What's strange?" inquired Elai. "I see nothing strange..."

"Look," said Ulan Dhor, "by that pillar. Do you see that man in the green cloak?"

She glanced at him in puzzlement. "There is no man there."

"There is a man there," said Ulan Dhor. "Look again."

She laughed. "You are joking...or can you see ghosts?"

Ulan Dhor shook his head in defeat. "You are the victims of some powerful magic."

She led him to one of the flowing roadways; as they were carried through the city he noticed a boat-shaped hull built of bright metal with four wheels and a transparent-domed compartment.

He pointed. "What is that?"

"It is a magic car. When a certain lever is pressed the wizardry of the older times gives it great speed. Rash young men ride them along the streets... See there," and she pointed to a somewhat similar hull toppled into the basin of a long, dry fountain. "That is another one of the ancient wonders — a craft with the power to fly through the air. There are many of them scattered through the city — on the towers, on high terraces, and sometimes, like this one, fallen into the streets."

"And no one flies them?" asked Ulan Dhor curiously.

"We are all afraid."

Ulan Dhor thought, what a marvel to own one of these air-cars! He stepped off the flowing road.

"Where are you going?" asked Elai anxiously, coming after him.

"I wish to examine one of these air-cars."

"Be careful, Ulan Dhor. They are said to be dangerous..."

Ulan Dhor peered through the transparent dome, saw a cushioned seat, a series of little levers inscribed with characters strange to him and a large knurled ball mounted on a metal rod.

He said to the girl, "Those are evidently the guides to the mechanism... How does one enter such a car?"

She said doubtfully, "This button will perhaps release the dome." She pressed a knob; the dome snapped back, releasing a puff of stagnant air.

"Now," said Ulan Dhor, "I will experiment." He reached within, turned down a switch. Nothing happened.

"Be careful, Ulan Dhor!" breathed the girl. "Beware of magic!"

Ulan Dhor twisted a knob. The car quivered. He touched another lever. The boat made a curious whining sound, jerked. The dome began to settle. Ulan Dhor snatched back his arm. The dome snapped into place over a fold of his gray cloak. The boat jerked again, made a sudden movement, and Ulan Dhor was dragged willy-nilly after.

Elai cried out, seized his ankles. Cursing, Ulan Dhor dropped out of his cloak, watched while the air-boat took a wild uncontrolled curvet, crashed against the side of a tower. It fell with another clang of colliding metal and stone.

"Next time," said Ulan Dhor, "I will..."

He became aware of a strange pressure in the air. He turned. Elai was staring at him, hand against her mouth, eyes screwed up as if she were repressing a scream.

Ulan Dhor glanced around the streets. The slowly moving people, Grays and Greens, had vanished. The streets were empty.

"Elai," said Ulan Dhor, "why do you look at me like that?"

"The red, in daylight — and the color of Pansiu on your legs — it is our death, our death!"

"By no means," said Ulan Dhor cheerfully. "Not while I wear my sword and..."

A stone, coming from nowhere, crashed into the ground at his feet. He looked right and left for his assailant, nostrils flaring in anger.

In vain. The doorways, the arcades, the porticos were bare and empty.

Another stone, large as his fist, struck him between the

shoulder-blades. He sprang around and saw only the crumbled facade of ancient Ampridatvir, the empty street, the glistening gliding strip.

A stone hissed six inches from Elai's head, and at the same instant another struck his thigh.

Ulan Dhor recognized defeat. He could not fight stones with his sword. "We had better retreat..." He ducked a great paving block that would have split his skull.

"Back to the strip," the girl said in a dull and helpless voice. "We can take refuge across the square." A stone, looping idly down, struck her cheek; she cried in pain and fell to her knees.

Ulan Dhor snarled like an animal and sought men to kill. But no living person, man, woman, or child, was visible, though the stones continued to hurtle at his head.

He stooped, picked up Elai and ran to the swift central flow of the strip.

The rain of stones presently halted. The girl opened her eyes, winced, and shut them again. "Everything whirls," she whispered. "I have gone mad. Almost I might think —"

Ulan Dhor thought to recognize the tower where he had spent the night. He stepped off the strip and approached the portico. He was wrong; a crystal plane barred him the tower. As he hesitated, it melted at a spot directly in front of him and formed a doorway. Ulan Dhor stared wonderingly. Further magic of the ancient builders.

It was impersonal magic, and harmless. Ulan Dhor stepped through. The doorway dwindled, fused, and became clear crystal behind him.

The hall was bare and cold, though the walls were rich with colored metals and gorgeous enamel. A mural decorated one wall — men and women in flowing clothes were depicted tending flowers in gardens curiously bright and sunny, playing airy games, dancing.

Very beautiful, thought Ulan Dhor, but no place to defend himself against attack. Passageways to either side were echoing and empty; ahead was a small chamber with a floor of glimmering floss, which seemed to radiate light. He stepped within. His feet rose from the floor; he floated, lighter than thistle-down. Elai no longer weighed in his arms. He gave an involuntary hoarse call, struggled to return his feet to ground, without success.

He floated upward like a leaf wafted in the wind. Ulan Dhor prepared himself for the sickening plunge when the magic quieted. But the floors fell past, and the ground level became ever more distant. A marvellous spell, thought Ulan Dhor grimly, thus to rob a man of his footing; how soon would the force relax and dash them to their deaths?

"Reach out," said Elai faintly. "Take hold of the bar."

He leaned far over, seized the railing, drew them to a landing, and, disbelieving his own safety, stepped into an apartment of several rooms. Crumbled heaps of dust were all that remained of the furniture.

He lay Elai on the soft floor; she raised her hand to her face and smiled wanly. "Ooh — it hurts."

Ulan Dhor watched with a strange sense of weakness and lassitude.

Elai said, "I don't know what we will do now. There is no longer a home for me; so shall we starve, for no one will give us food."

Ulan Dhor laughed sourly. "We will never lack for food — not while the keeper of a green booth can not see a man in a gray cloak ... But there are other things more important — the tablets of Rogol Domedonfors — and they seem completely inaccessible."

She said earnestly, "You would be killed. The men in red must fight everyone — as you saw today. And even if you reached the Temple of Pansiu, there are pitfalls, traps, poison stakes, and the ghosts on guard."

"Ghosts? Nonsense. They are men, exactly like the Grays, except that they wear green. Your brain refuses to see men in green ... I have heard of such things, such obstructions of the mind ..."

She said in an injured tone, "No other Grays see them. Perhaps it is you who suffers the hallucinations."

"Perhaps," agreed Ulan Dhor with a wry grin. They sat for a space in the dusty stillness of the old tower, then Ulan Dhor sat forward, clasped his knees, frowning. Lethargy was the precursor of defeat. "We must consider this Temple of Pansiu."

"We shall be killed," she said simply.

Ulan Dhor, already in better spirits, said, "You should practice optimism ... Where can I find another air-car?"

She stared at him. "Surely you are a madman!"

Ulan Dhor rose to his feet. "Where may one be found?"

She shook her head. "You are resolved on death, one way or another."

She rose also. "We will ascend the Shaft of No-weight to the tower's highest level."

Without hesitation she stepped into the void, and Ulan Dhor gingerly followed. To the dizziest height they floated, and the walls of the shaft converged to a point far below. At the topmost landing they pulled themselves to solidity, stepped out on a terrace high up in the clean winds. Higher than the central mountains they stood, and the streets of Ampridatvir were gray threads far below. The harbor was a basin, and the sea spread away into the haze at the horizon.

Three air-cars rested on the terrace, and the metal was as bright, the glass as clear, the enamel as vivid as if the cars had just dropped from the sky.

They went to the nearest; Ulan Dhor pressed the entry button, and the dome slid back with a thin dry hiss of friction.

The interior was like that of the other car — a long cushioned seat, a globe mounted on a rod, a number of switches. The cloth of the seat crackled with age as Ulan Dhor prodded it with his hand, and the trapped air smelt very stale. He stepped inside, and Elai followed. "I will accompany you; death by falling is faster than starvation, and less painful than the rocks ..."

"I hope we will neither fall nor starve," replied Ulan Dhor. Cautiously he touched the switches, ready to throw them back at any dangerous manifestation.

The dome snapped over their heads; relays thousands of years old meshed, cams twisted, shafts plunged home. The air-car jerked, lofted up into the red and dark blue sky. Ulan Dhor grasped the globe, found how to turn the boat, how to twist the nose up or down. This was pure joy, intoxication — wonderful mastery of the air! It was easier than he had imagined. It was easier than walking. He tried all the handles and switches, found how to hover, drop, brake. He found the speed handle and pushed it far over, and the wind sang past the air-boat. Far over the sea they flew, until the island was blue loom at the rim of the world. Low and high — skimming the wave crests, plunging through the magenta wisps of the upper clouds.

Elai sat relaxed, calm, exalted. She had changed; she seemed closer to Ulan Dhor than to Ampridatvir; some subtle tie had been cut.

"Let's go on," she said. "On and on and on — across the world, past the forests..."

Ulan Dhor glanced at her sideways. She was very beautiful now — cleaner, finer, stronger than the women he had known in Kaiin. He said regretfully, "Then we would starve indeed — for neither of us has the craft to survive in the wilderness. And I am bound to seek the tablets..."

She sighed. "Very well. We will be killed. What does it matter? All Earth dies..."

Evening came, and they returned to Ampridatvir. "There," said Elai, "there is the Temple of Cazdal and there the Temple of Pansiu."

Ulan Dhor dropped the boat low over the Temple of Pansiu. "Where is the entrance?"

"Through the arch — and every place holds a different danger."

"But we fly," Ulan Dhor reminded her.

He lowered the boat ten feet above the ground and slid it through the arch.

Guided by a dim light ahead, Ulan Dhor maneuvered the boat down the dark passage, through another arch; and they were in the nave.

The podium where the tablet sat was like the citadel of a walled city. The first obstacle was a wide pit, backed by a glassy wall. Then there was a moat of sulfur-colored liquid, and beyond, in an open space, five men kept a torpid watch. Undetected Ulan Dhor moved the boat through the upper shadows and halted directly over the podium.

"Ready now," he muttered, and grounded the boat. The glistening tablet was almost within reach. He raised the dome; Elai leaned out, seized the tablet. The five guards gave an anguished roar, rushed forward.

"Back!" cried Ulan Dhor. He warded off a flying spear with his sword. She drew back with the tablet, Ulan Dhor slammed the dome. The guards leapt on the ship, clawing at the smooth metal, beating at it with their fists. The ship rose high; one by one they lost their grip, fell screaming to the floor.

Back through the arch, down the black passageway, through the entrance and out into the dark sky. Behind them a great horn set up a crazy clangor.

Ulan Dhor examined his prize — an oval sheet of transparent substance bearing a dozen lines of meaningless marks.

"We have won!" said Elai raptly. "You are the Lord of Ampridatvir!"

"Half yet remains," said Ulan Dhor. "There is still the tablet in the Temple of Cazdal."

"But — it is madness! Already you have —"

"One is useless without the other."

Her wild arguments subsided only as they hovered over the arch into Cazdal's Temple.

As the boat glided through the dark gap it struck a thread which dropped a great load of stones from a chute. The first of these, striking the sloping side of the air-car, buffeted it away. Ulan Dhor cursed. The guards would be alert and watchful.

He drifted along at the very top of the passage, hidden in the murk. Presently two guards, bearing torches and careful of their steps, came to investigate the sound. They passed directly below the boat, and Ulan Dhor hastened forward, through the arch into the nave. As in the Temple of Pansiu, the tablet gleamed in the middle of a fortress.

The guards were wide awake, nervously watching the opening.

"Boldness, now!" said Ulan Dhor. He sent the boat darting across the walls and pits and seething moat, settled beside the podium, snapped the dome back, sprang out. He seized the tablet as the guards came roaring forward, spears extended. The foremost flung his spear; Ulan Dhor struck it down and tossed the tablet into the boat.

But they were upon him; he would be impaled if he sought to climb within the boat. He sprang forward, hewed off the shaft of one spear, chopped at one man's shoulder on the back-sweep, seized the shaft of the third spear, and pulled the man into range of his sword point. The third guard fell back, shouting for help. Ulan Dhor turned, leapt into the boat. The guard rushed forward, Ulan Dhor whirled and met him with the point of his sword in his cheek. Spouting blood and wailing hysterically, the guard fell back. Ulan Dhor threw the lift lever; the boat rose high and moved toward the opening.

And presently the alarm horn at Cazdal's Temple was adding its harsh yell to the sound from across the city.

The boat drifted slowly through the sky.

"Look!" said Elai, grasping his arm. By torchlight men and women crowded and milled in the streets — Greens and Grays, panicked by the message of the horns.

Elai gasped. "Ulan Dhor! I see! I see! The men in Green! Is it possible... Have they always been..."

"The brain-spell has broken," said Ulan Dhor, "and not only for you. Below they see each other, too..."

For the first time in memory, Greens and Grays looked at each other. Their faces twisted, contorted. In the flicker of torches Ulan Dhor saw them drawing back in revulsion from each other, and heard the tumult of their cries: "Demon!... Demon!... Gray ghost!... Vile Green Demon!..."

Thousands of obsessed torch-bearers sidled past each other, glowering, reviling each other, screaming in hate and fear. They were all mad, he thought — tangled, constricted of brain...

As by a secret signal, the crowd seethed into battle, and the hateful yells curdled Ulan Dhor's blood. Elai turned sobbing away. Terrible work was done, on men, women, children — no matter who the victim, if he wore the opposite color.

A louder snarling arose at the edge of the mob — a joyful sound, and a dozen shambling Gauns appeared, towering above the Greens and Grays. They rended, tore, ripped, and insane hate melted before insane fear. Greens and Grays separated, and ran to their homes, and the Gauns roamed the streets alone.

Ulan Dhor tore his glance away and held his forehead. "Was this my doing?... Was this a deed of mine?"

"Sooner or later it would have happened," said Elai dully. "Unless Earth waned and died first..."

Ulan Dhor picked up the two tablets. "And here is what I sought to attain — the tablets of Rogol Domedonfors. They pulled me a thousand leagues across the Melantine; I have them in my hands now, and they are like worthless shards of glass..."

The boat floated high, and Ampridatvir became a setting of pale crystals in the starlight. In the luminescence of the instrument panel, Ulan Dhor fitted the two tablets together. The marks merged, became characters, and the characters bore the words of the ancient magician:

Faithless children — Rogol Domedonfors dies, and so lives forever in the Ampridatvir he has loved and served! When intelligence and good will restore order to the city; or when blood and steel teaches the folly of bridled credulity and passion, and all but the toughest dead: — then shall these tablets be read. And I say to him who reads it, go to the Tower of Fate with the yellow dome, ascend to the topmost floor, show red to the left eye of Rogol Domedonfors, yellow to the right eye, and then blue to both; do this, I say, and share the power of Rogol Domedonfors.

Ulan Dhor asked, "Where is the Tower of Fate?"

Elai shook her head. "There is Rodeil's Tower, and the Red Tower and the Tower of the Screaming Ghost, and the Tower of Trumpets and the Bird's Tower, and the Tower of Gauns — but I know of no Tower of Fate."

"Which tower has a yellow dome?"

"I don't know."

"We will search in the morning."

"In the morning," she said leaning against him drowsily.

"The morning..." said Ulan Dhor, fondling her yellow hair.

When the old red sun rose, they drifted back over the city and found the people of Ampridatvir awake before them, intent on murder.

The fighting and the killing was not so wild as the night before. It was a craftier slaughter. Stealthy groups of men waylaid stragglers, or broke into houses to strangle women and children.

Ulan Dhor muttered, "Soon there will be none left in Ampridatvir upon whom to work Rogol Domedonfors' power." He turned to Elai. "Have you no father, no mother, for whom you fear?"

She shook her head. "I have lived my life with a dull and tyrannical uncle."

Ulan Dhor turned away. He saw a yellow dome; no other was visible: The Tower of Fate.

"There." He pointed, turned down the nose of the air-car.

Parking on a high level, they entered the dusty corridors, found an anti-gravity shaft, and rose to the topmost floor. Here they found a small chamber, decorated with vivid murals. The scene was a court of ancient Ampridatvir. Men and women in colored silks conversed and banqueted and, in the central plaque, paid homage to a patriarchal ruler with a rugged chin, burning eyes, and a white beard. He was clad in a purple and black gown and sat on a carved chair.

"Rogol Domedonfors!" murmured Elai, and the room held its breath, grew still. They felt the stir their living breath made in the long-quiet air, and the depicted eyes stared deep into their brains...

Ulan Dhor said, " 'Red to the left eye, yellow to the right; then blue to both.' Well — there are blue tiles in the hall, and I wear a red coat."

They found blue and yellow tiles, and Ulan Dhor cut a strip from the hem of his tunic.

Red to the left eye, yellow to the right. Blue to both. A click, a screech, a whirring like a hundred bee-hives.

The wall opened on a flight of steps. Ulan Dhor entered, and, with Elai breathing hard at his back, mounted the steps.

They came out in a flood of daylight, under the dome itself. In the center on a pedestal sat a glistening round-topped cylinder, black and vitreous.

The whirring rose to a shrill whine. The cylinder quivered, softened, became barely transparent, slumped a trifle. In the center hung a pulpy white mass — a brain?

The cylinder was alive.

It sprouted pseudopods which poised wavering in the air. Ulan Dhor and Elai watched frozen, close together. One black finger shaped itself to an eye, another formed a mouth. The eye inspected them carefully.

The mouth said cheerfully, "Greetings across time, greetings. So you have come at last to rouse old Rogol Domedonfors from his dreams? I have dreamed long and well — but it seems for an unconscionable period. How long? Twenty years? Fifty years? Let me look."

The eye swung to a tube on the wall, a quarter full of gray powder.

The mouth gave a cry of wonder. "The energy has nearly dissipated! How long have I slept? With a half-life of 1,200 years — over five thousand years!" The eye swung back to Ulan Dhor and Elai. "Who are you then? Where are my bickering subjects, the adherents of Pansiu and Cazdal? Did they kill themselves then, so long ago?"

"No," said Ulan Dhor with a sick grin. "They are still fighting in the streets."

The eye-tentacle extended swiftly, thrust through a window, and looked down over the city. The central jelly twitched, became suffused with an orange glow. The voice spoke again, and it held a terrible harshness. Ulan Dhor's neck tingled and he felt Elai's hand clenching deep into his arm.

"Five thousand years!" cried the voice. "Five thousand years and the wretches still quarrel? Time has taught them no wisdom? Then stronger agencies must be used. Rogol Domedonfors will show them wisdom. Behold!"

A vast sound came from below, a hundred sharp reports. Ulan Dhor and Elai hastened to the window and looked down. A mind-filling sight occupied the streets.

The ten-foot vestibules leading below the city had snapped open. From each of these licked a great tentacle of black transparent jelly like the substance of the fluid roads.

The tentacles reached into the air, sprouted a hundred branches which pursued the madly fleeing Ampridatvians, caught them, stripped away their robes of gray and green, then whipping them high through the air, dropped them into the great central square. In the chill morning air the populace of Ampridatvir stood mingled naked together and no man could distinguish Green from Gray.

"Rogol Domedonfors has great long arms now," cried a vast voice, "strong as the moon, all-seeing as the air."

The voice came from everywhere, nowhere.

"I am Rogol Domedonfors, the last ruler of Ampridatvir. And to this state have you descended? Dwellers in hovels, eaters of filth? Watch — in a moment I repair the neglect of five thousand years!"

The tentacles sprouted a thousand appendages — hard horny cutters, nozzles that spouted blue flame, tremendous scoops, and each appendage sprouted an eye-stalk. These ranged the city, and wherever there was crumbling or mark of age the tentacles dug, tore, blasted, burnt; then spewed new materials into place, and when they passed, new and gleaming structures remained behind.

Many-armed tentacles gathered the litter of ages; when loaded they snapped high through the air, a monstrous catapult, flinging the rubbish far out over the sea. And wherever was gray paint or green paint a tentacle ground off the color, sprayed new various pigments.

Down every street ran the tremendous root-things and off-shoots plunged into every tower, every dwelling, every park and square — demolishing, stripping, building, clearing, repairing. Ampridatvir was gripped and permeated by Rogol Domedonfors as a tree's roots clench the ground.

In a time measured by breaths, a new Ampridatvir had replaced the ruins, a gleaming, glistening city — proud, intrepid, challenging the red sun.

Ulan Dhor and Elai had watched in a half-conscious, uncomprehending daze. Was it possibly reality; was there such a being which could demolish a city and build it anew while a man watched?

Arms of black jelly darted over the hills of the island, threaded the caves where the Gauns lay gorged and torpid. It seized, snatched them through the air, and dangled them above the huddled Ampridatvians — a hundred Gauns on a hundred tentacles, horrible fruits on a weird tree.

"Look!" boomed a voice, boastful and wild. "These whom you have feared! See how Rogol Domedonfors deals with these!"

The tentacles flicked, and a hundred Gauns hurtled — sprawling, wheeling shapes — high over Ampridatvir; and they fell far out in the sea.

"The creature is mad," whispered Ulan Dhor to Elai. "The long dreaming has addled its brain."

"Behold the new Ampridatvir!" boomed the mighty voice. "See it for the first and last time. For now you die! You have proved unworthy of the past — unworthy to worship the new god Rogol Domedonfors. There are two here beside me who shall found the new race —"

Ulan Dhor started in alarm. What? He to live in Ampridatvir under the thumb of the mad super-being?

No.

And perhaps he would never be so close to the brain again.

With a single motion he drew his sword and hurled it point-first into the translucent cylinder of jelly — transfixed the brain, skewered it on the shaft of steel.

The most awful sound yet heard on Earth shattered the air. Men and women went mad in the square.

Rogol Domedonfors' city-girding tentacles beat up and down in frantic agony, as an injured insect lashes his legs. The gorgeous towers toppled. The Ampridatvians fled shrieking through cataclysm.

Ulan Dhor and Elai ran for the terrace where they had left the air-car. Behind they heard a hoarse whisper — a broken voice.

"I — am not — dead — yet! If all else, if all dreams are broken — I will kill you two..."

They tumbled into the air-car. Ulan Dhor threw it into the air. By a terrible effort a tentacle stopped its mad thrashing and jerked up to intercept them. Ulan Dhor swerved, plunged off through the sky. The tentacle darted to cut them off.

Ulan Dhor pressed hard down on the speed lever, and air whined and sang behind the craft. And directly behind came the wavering black arm of the dying god, straining to touch the fleeting midge that had so hurt it.

"More! More!" prayed Ulan Dhor to the air-car.

"Go higher," whispered the girl. "Higher — faster —"

Ulan Dhor tilted the nose; up on a slant flashed the car, and the straining arm followed behind — a tremendous member stretching rigid through the sky, a black rainbow footed in distant Ampridatvir.

Rogol Domedonfors died. The arm snapped into a wisp of smoke and slowly sank toward the sea.

Ulan Dhor held his boat at full speed until the island disappeared across the horizon. He slowed, sighed, relaxed.

Elai suddenly flung herself against his shoulder and burst into hysteria.

"Quiet, girl, quiet," admonished Ulan Dhor. "We are safe; we are forever done of the cursed city."

She quieted; presently: "Where do we go now?"

Ulan Dhor's eyes roved about the air-car with doubt and calculation. "There will be no magic for Kandive. However, I will have a great tale to tell him, and he may be satisfied... He will surely want the air-car. But I will contrive, I will contrive..."

She whispered, "Cannot we fly to the east, and fly and fly and fly, till we find where the sun rises, and perhaps a quiet meadow where there are fruit trees…"

Ulan Dhor looked to the south and thought of Kaiin with its quiet nights and wine-colored days, the wide palace where he made his home, and the couch from which he could look out over Sanreale Bay, the ancient olive trees, the harlequinade festival-times.

He said, "Elai, you will like Kaiin."

VI

Guyal of Sfere

GUYAL OF SFERE HAD BEEN BORN one apart from his fellows and early proved a source of vexation for his sire. Normal in outward configuration, there existed within his mind a void which ached for nourishment. It was as if a spell had been cast upon his birth, a harassment visited on the child in a spirit of sardonic mockery, so that every occurrence, no matter how trifling, became a source of wonder and amazement. Even as young as four seasons he was expounding such inquiries as:

"Why do squares have more sides than triangles?"

"How will we see when the sun goes dark?"

"Do flowers grow under the ocean?"

"Do stars hiss and sizzle when rain comes by night?"

To which his impatient sire gave such answers as:

"So it was ordained by the Pragmatica; squares and triangles must obey the rote."

"We will be forced to grope and feel our way."

"I have never verified this matter; only the Curator would know."

"By no means, since the stars are high above the rain, higher even than the highest clouds, and swim in rarified air where rain will never breed."

As Guyal grew to youth, this void in his mind, instead of becoming limp and waxy, seemed to throb with a more violent ache. And so he asked:

"Why do people die when they are killed?"

"Where does beauty vanish when it goes?"

"How long have men lived on Earth?"

"What is beyond the sky?"

To which his sire, biting acerbity back from his lips, would respond:

"Death is the heritage of life; a man's vitality is like air in a bladder. Poinct this bubble and away, away, away, flees life, like the color of fading dream."

"Beauty is a luster which love bestows to guile the eye. Therefore it may be said that only when the brain is without love will the eye look and see no beauty."

"Some say men rose from the earth like grubs in a corpse; others aver that the first men desired residence and so created Earth by sorcery. The question is shrouded in technicality; only the Curator may answer with exactness."

"An endless waste."

And Guyal pondered and postulated, proposed and expounded until he found himself the subject of surreptitious humor. The demesne was visited by a rumor that a gleft, coming upon Guyal's mother in labor, had stolen part of Guyal's brain, which deficiency he now industriously sought to restore.

Guyal therefore drew himself apart and roamed the grassy hills of Sfere in solitude. But ever was his mind acquisitive, ever did he seek to exhaust the lore of all around him, until at last his father in vexation refused to hear further inquiries, declaring that all knowledge had been known, that the trivial and useless had been discarded, leaving a residue which was all that was necessary to a sound man.

At this time Guyal was in his first manhood, a slight but well-knit youth with wide clear eyes, a penchant for severely elegant dress, and a hidden trouble which showed itself in the clamps at the corner of his mouth.

Hearing his father's angry statement Guyal said, "One more question, then I ask no more."

"Speak," declared his father. "One more question I grant you."

"You have often referred me to the Curator; who is he, and where may I find him, so as to allay my ache for knowledge?"

A moment the father scrutinized the son, whom he now considered past the verge of madness. Then he responded in a quiet voice, "The Curator guards the Museum of Man, which antique legend places in the Land of the Falling Wall — beyond the mountains of Fer Aquila and north of Ascolais. It is not certain that either Curator or Museum still exist; still it would seem that if the Curator knows all things, as is the legend, then surely he would know the wizardly foil to death."

Guyal said, "I would seek the Curator, and the Museum of Man, that I likewise may know all things."

The father said with patience, "I will bestow on you my fine white horse, my Expansible Egg for your shelter, my Scintillant Dagger to illuminate the night. In addition, I lay a blessing along the trail, and danger will slide you by so long as you never wander from the trail."

Guyal quelled the hundred new questions at his tongue, including an inquisition as to where his father had learned these manifestations of sorcery, and accepted the gifts: the horse, the magic shelter, the dagger with the luminous pommel, and the blessing to guard him from the disadvantageous circumstances which plagued travelers along the dim trails of Ascolais.

He caparisoned the horse, honed the dagger, cast a last glance around the old manse at Sfere, and set forth to the north, with the void in his mind athrob for the soothing pressure of knowledge.

He ferried the River Scaum on an old barge. Aboard the barge and so off the trail, the blessing lost its puissance and the barge-tender, who coveted Guyal's rich accoutrements, sought to cudgel him with a knob-lolly. Guyal fended off the blow and kicked the man into the murky deep, where he drowned.

Mounting the north bank of the Scaum he saw ahead the Porphiron Scar, the dark poplars and white columns of Kaiin, the dull gleam of Sanreale Bay.

Wandering the crumbled streets, he put the languid inhabitants such a spate of questions that one in wry jocularity commended him to a professional augur.

This one dwelled in a booth painted with the Signs of the Aumoklopelastianic Cabal. He was a lank brownman with red-rimmed eyes and a stained white beard.

"What are your fees?" inquired Guyal cautiously.

"I respond to three questions," stated the augur. "For twenty terces I phrase the answer in clear and actionable language; for ten I use the language of cant, which occasionally admits of ambiguity; for five, I speak a parable which you must interpret as you will; and for one terce, I babble in an unknown tongue."

"First I must inquire, how profound is your knowledge?"

"I know all," responded the augur. "The secrets of red and the secrets of black, the lost spells of Grand Motholam, the way of the fish and the voice of the bird."

"And where have you learned all these things?"

"By pure induction," explained the augur. "I retire into my booth, I closet myself with never a glint of light, and, so sequestered, I resolve the profundities of the world."

"With all this precious knowledge at hand," ventured Guyal, "why do you live so meagerly, with not an ounce of fat to your frame and these miserable rags to your back?"

The augur stood back in fury. "Go along, go along! Already I have wasted fifty terces of wisdom on you, who have never a copper to your pouch. If you desire free enlightenment," and he cackled in mirth, "seek out the Curator." And he sheltered himself in his booth.

Guyal took lodging for the night, and in the morning continued north. The ravaged acres of the Old Town passed to his left, and the trail took to the fabulous forest.

For many a day Guyal rode north, and, heedful of danger, held to the trail. By night he surrounded himself and his horse in his magical habiliment, the Expansible Egg — a membrane impermeable to thew, claw, ensorcelment, pressure, sound and chill — and so rested at ease despite the efforts of the avid creatures of the dark.

The great dull globe of the sun fell behind him; the days became wan and the nights bitter, and at last the crags of Fer Aquila showed as a tracing on the north horizon.

The forest had become lower and less dense, and the characteristic tree was the daobado, a rounded massy construction of heavy gnarled branches, these a burnished russet bronze, clumped with dark balls of foliage. Beside a giant of the species Guyal came upon a village of turf huts. A gaggle of surly louts appeared and surrounded him with expressions of curiosity. Guyal, no less than the villagers, had questions to ask, but none would speak till the hetman strode up — a burly man who wore a shaggy fur hat, a cloak of brown fur and a bristling beard, so that it was hard to see where one ended and the other began. He exuded a rancid odor which displeased Guyal, who, from motives of courtesy, kept his distaste concealed.

"Where go you?" asked the hetman.

"I wish to cross the mountains to the Museum of Man," said Guyal. "Which way does the trail lead?"

The hetman pointed out a notch on the silhouette of the mountains. "There is Omona Gap, which is the shortest and best route, though there is no trail. None comes and none goes, since when you pass the Gap, you walk an unknown land. And with no traffic there manifestly need be no trail."

The news did not cheer Guyal.

"How then is it known that Omona Gap is on the way to the Museum?"

The hetman shrugged. "Such is our tradition."

Guyal turned his head at a hoarse snuffling and saw a pen of woven wattles. In a litter of filth and matted straw stood a number of hulking men eight or nine feet tall. They were naked, with shocks of dirty yellow hair and watery blue eyes. They had waxy faces and expressions of crass stupidity. As Guyal watched, one of them ambled to a trough and noisily began gulping gray mash.

Guyal said, "What manner of things are these?"

The hetman blinked in amusement at Guyal's naïveté. "Those are our oasts, naturally." And he gestured in disapprobation at Guyal's white horse. "Never have I seen a stranger oast than the one you bestride. Ours carry us easier and appear to be less vicious; in addition no flesh is more delicious than oast properly braised and kettled."

Standing close, he fondled the metal of Guyal's saddle and the red and yellow embroidered quilt. "Your deckings however are rich and of superb quality. I will therefore bestow you my large and weighty oast in return for this creature with its accoutrements."

Guyal politely declared himself satisfied with his present mount, and the hetman shrugged his shoulders.

A horn sounded. The hetman looked about, then turned back to Guyal. "Food is prepared; will you eat?"

Guyal glanced toward the oast-pen. "I am not presently hungry, and I must hasten forward. However, I am grateful for your kindness."

He departed; as he passed under the arch of the great daobado, he turned a glance back toward the village. There seemed an unwonted activity among the huts. Remembering the hetman's covetous touch at his saddle, and aware that no longer did he ride the protected trail, Guyal urged his horse forward and pounded fast under the trees.

As he neared the foothills the forest dwindled to a savannah, floored with a dull, jointed grass that creaked under the horse's hooves. Guyal glanced up and down the plain. The sun, old and red as an autumn pomegranate, wallowed in the south-west; the light across the plain was dim and watery; the mountains presented a curiously artificial aspect, like a tableau planned for the effect of eery desolation.

Guyal glanced once again at the sun. Another hour of light, then the dark night of the latter-day Earth. Guyal twisted in the saddle, looked behind him, feeling lone, solitary, vulnerable. Four oasts, carrying men on their shoulders, came trotting from the forest. Sighting Guyal, they broke into a lumbering run. With a crawling skin Guyal wheeled his horse and eased the reins, and the white horse loped across the plain toward Omona Gap. Behind came the oasts, bestraddled by the fur-cloaked villagers.

As the sun touched the horizon, another forest ahead showed as an indistinct line of murk. Guyal looked back to his pursuers, bounding now a mile behind, turned his gaze back to the forest. An ill place to ride by night...

The darkling foliage loomed above him; he passed under the first gnarled boughs. If the oasts were unable to sniff out a trail, they might now be eluded. He changed directions, turned once, twice, a third time, then stood his horse to listen. Far away a crashing in the brake reached his ears. Guyal dismounted, led the horse into a deep hollow where a bank of foliage made a screen. Presently the four men on their hulking oasts passed in the afterglow above him, black double-shapes in attitudes suggestive of ill-temper and disappointment.

The thud and pad of feet dwindled and died.

The horse moved restlessly; the foliage rustled.

A damp air passed down the hollow and chilled the back of Guyal's neck. Darkness rose from old Earth like ink in a basin.

Guyal shivered: best to ride away through the forest, away from the dour villagers and their numb mounts. Away...

He turned his horse up to the height where the four had passed and sat listening. Far down the wind he heard a hoarse call. Turning in the opposite direction he let the horse choose its own path.

Branches and boughs knit patterns on the fading purple over him; the air smelt of moss and dank mould. The horse stopped short. Guyal, tensing in every muscle, leaned a little forward, head twisted, listening. There was a feel of danger on his cheek. The air was still, uncanny; his eyes could plumb not ten feet into the black. Somewhere near was death — grinding, roaring death, to come as a sudden shock.

Sweating cold, afraid to stir a muscle, he forced himself to dismount. Stiffly he slid from the saddle, brought forth the Expansible Egg, and flung it around his horse and himself. Ah, now... Guyal released the pressure of his breath. Safety.

Wan red light slanted through the branches from the east. Guyal's breath steamed in the air when he emerged from the Egg. After a handful of dried fruit for himself and a sack of meal for the horse, he mounted and set out toward the mountains.

The forest passed, and Guyal rode out on an upland. He scanned the line of mountains. Suffused with rose sunlight, the gray, sage green, dark green range rambled far to the west toward the Melantine, far to the east into the Falling Wall country. Where was Omona Gap?

Guyal of Sfere searched in vain for the notch which had been visible from the village of the fur-cloaked murderers.

He frowned and turned his eyes up the height of the mountains. Weathered by the rains of earth's duration, the slopes were easy and the crags rose like the stumps of rotten teeth. Guyal turned his horse uphill and rode the trackless slope into the mountains of Fer Aquila.

Guyal of Sfere had lost his way in a land of wind and naked crags. As night came he slouched numbly in the saddle while his horse took him where it would. Somewhere the ancient way through Omona Gap led to the northern tundra, but now, under a chilly overcast, north, east, south and west were alike under the lavender-metal sky. Guyal reined his horse and, rising in the saddle, searched the landscape. The crags rose, tall, remote; the ground was barren of all but clumps of dry shrub. He slumped back in the saddle, and his white horse jogged forward.

Head bowed to the wind rode Guyal, and the mountains slanted along the twilight like the skeleton of a fossil god.

The horse halted, and Guyal found himself at the brink of a wide valley. The wind had died; the valley was quiet. Guyal leaned forward staring. Below spread a dark and lifeless city. Mist blew along the streets and the afterglow fell dull on slate roofs.

The horse snorted and scraped the stony ground.

"A strange town," said Guyal, "with no lights, no sound, no smell of smoke... Doubtless an abandoned ruin from ancient times..."

He debated descending to the streets. At times the old ruins were haunted by peculiar distillations, but such a ruin might be joined to the tundra by a trail. With this thought in mind he started his horse down the slope.

He entered the town and the hooves rang loud and sharp on the cobbles. The buildings were framed of stone and dark mortar and seemed in uncommonly good preservation. A few lintels had cracked and sagged, a few walls gaped open, but for the most part the stone houses had successfully met the gnaw of time... Guyal scented smoke. Did people live here still? He would proceed with caution.

Before a building which seemed to be a hostelry flowers bloomed in an urn. Guyal reined his horse and reflected that flowers were rarely cherished by persons of hostile disposition.

"Hallo!" he called — once, twice.

No heads peered from the doors, no orange flicker brightened the windows. Guyal slowly turned and rode on.

The street widened and twisted toward a large hall, where Guyal saw a light. The building had a high facade, broken by four large windows, each of which had its two blinds of patined bronze filigree, and each overlooked a small balcony. A marble balustrade fronting the terrace shimmered bone-white, and, behind, the hall's portal of massive wood stood slightly ajar; from here came the beam of light and also a strain of music.

Guyal of Sfere, halting, gazed not at the house nor at the light through the door. He dismounted and bowed to the young woman who sat pensively along the course of the balustrade. Though it was very cold, she wore but a simple gown, yellow-orange, a daffodil's color. Topaz hair fell loose to her shoulders and gave her face a cast of gravity and thoughtfulness.

As Guyal straightened from his greeting the woman nodded, smiled slightly, and absently fingered the hair by her cheek.

"A bitter night for travelers."

"A bitter night for musing on the stars," responded Guyal.

She smiled again. "I am not cold. I sit and dream... I listen to the music."

"What place is this?" inquired Guyal, looking up the street, down the street, and once more to the girl. "Are there any here but yourself?"

"This is Carchasel," said the girl, "abandoned by all ten thousand years ago. Only I and my aged uncle live here, finding this place a refuge from the Saponids of the tundra."

Guyal thought: this woman may or may not be a witch.

"You are cold and weary," said the girl, "and I keep you standing in the street." She rose to her feet. "Our hospitality is yours."

"Which I gladly accept," said Guyal, "but first I must stable my horse."

"He will be content in the house yonder. We have no stable." Guyal, following her finger, saw a low stone building with a door opening into blackness.

He took the white horse thither and removed the bridle and saddle; then, standing in the doorway, he listened to the music he had noted before, the piping of a weird and ancient air.

"Strange, strange," he muttered, stroking the horse's muzzle. "The uncle plays music, the girl stares alone at the stars of the night..." He considered a moment. "I may be over suspicious. If witch she be, there is naught to be gained from me. If they be simple refugees as she says, and lovers of music, they may enjoy the airs from Ascolais; it will repay, in some measure, their hospitality." He reached into his saddlebag, brought forth his flute, and tucked it inside his jerkin.

He ran back to where the girl awaited him.

"You have not told me your name," she reminded him, "that I may introduce you to my uncle."

"I am Guyal of Sfere, by the River Scaum in Ascolais. And you?"

She smiled, pushing the portal wider. Warm yellow light fell into the cobbled street.

"I have no name. I need none. There has never been any but my uncle; and when he speaks, there is no one to answer but I."

Guyal stared in astonishment; then, deeming his wonder too apparent for courtesy, he controlled his expression. Perhaps she suspected him of wizardry and feared to pronounce her name lest he make magic with it.

They entered a flagged hall, and the sound of piping grew louder.

"I will call you Ameth, if I may," said Guyal. "That is a flower of the south, as golden and kind and fragrant as you seem to be."

She nodded. "You may call me Ameth."

They entered a tapestry-hung chamber, large and warm. A great fire glowed at one wall, and here stood a table bearing food. On a bench sat the musician — an old man, untidy, unkempt. His white hair hung tangled down his back; his beard, in no better case, was dirty and yellow. He wore a ragged kirtle, by no means clean, and the leather of his sandals had broken into dry cracks. Strangely, he did not take the flute from his mouth, but kept up his piping; and the girl in yellow, so Guyal noted, seemed to move in rhythm to the tones.

"Uncle Ludowik," she cried in a gay voice, "I bring you a guest, Sir Guyal of Sfere."

Guyal looked into the man's face and wondered. The eyes though somewhat rheumy with age, were gray and bright — feverishly bright and intelligent; and, so Guyal thought, awake with a strange joy. This joy further puzzled Guyal, for the lines of the face indicated nothing other than years of misery.

"Perhaps you play?" inquired Ameth. "My uncle is a great musician, and this is his time for music. He has kept the routine for many years…" She turned and smiled at Ludowik the musician. Guyal nodded politely.

Ameth motioned to the bounteous table. "Eat, Guyal, and I will pour you wine. Afterwards perhaps you will play the flute for us."

"Gladly," said Guyal, and he noticed how the joy on Ludowik's face grew more apparent, quivering around the corners of his mouth.

He ate and Ameth poured him golden wine until his head went to reeling. And never did Ludowik cease his piping — now a tender melody of running water, again a grave tune that told of the lost ocean to the west, another time a simple melody such as a child might sing at his games. Guyal noted with wonder how Ameth fitted her mood to the music — grave and gay as the music led her. Strange! thought Guyal. But then — people thus isolated were apt to develop peculiar mannerisms, and they seemed kindly withal.

He finished his meal and stood erect, steadying himself against the table. Ludowik was playing a lilting tune, a melody of glass birds swinging round and round on a red string in the sunlight. Ameth came dancing over to him and stood close — very close — and he smelled the warm perfume of her loose golden hair. Her face was happy and wild… Peculiar how Ludowik watched so grimly, and yet without a word. Perhaps he misdoubted a stranger's intent. Still…

"Now," breathed Ameth, "perhaps you will play the flute; you are so strong and young." Then she said quickly, as she saw Guyal's eyes widen, "I mean you will play on the flute for old uncle Ludowik, and he will be happy and go off to bed — and then we will sit and talk far into the night."

"Gladly will I play the flute," said Guyal. Curse the tongue of his, at once so fluent and yet so numb. It was the wine. "Gladly will I play. I am accounted quite skillful at my home manse at Sfere."

He glanced at Ludowik, then stared at the expression of crazy gladness he had surprised. Marvellous that a man should be so fond of music.

"Then — play!" breathed Ameth, urging him a little toward Ludowik and the flute.

"Perhaps," suggested Guyal, "I had better wait till your uncle pauses. I would seem discourteous —"

"No, as soon as you indicate that you wish to play, he will let off. Merely take the flute. You see," she confided, "he is rather deaf."

"Very well," said Guyal, "except that I have my own flute." And he brought it out from under his jerkin. "Why — what is the matter?" For a startling change had come over the girl and the old man. A quick light had risen in her eyes, and Ludowik's strange gladness had gone, and there was but dull hopelessness in his eyes, stupid resignation.

Guyal slowly stood back, bewildered. "Do you not wish me to play?"

There was a pause. "Of course," said Ameth, young and charming once more. "But I'm sure that Uncle Ludowik would enjoy hearing you play his flute. He is accustomed to the pitch — another scale might be unfamiliar..."

Ludowik nodded, and hope again shone in the rheumy old eyes. It was indeed a fine flute, Guyal saw, a rich piece of white metal, chased and set with gold, and Ludowik clutched this flute as if he would never let go.

"Take the flute," suggested Ameth. "He will not mind in the least." Ludowik shook his head, to signify the absence of his objections. But Guyal, noting with distaste the long stained beard, also shook his head. "I can play any scale, any tone on my flute. There is no need for me to use that of your uncle and possibly distress him. Listen," and he raised his instrument. "Here is a song of Kaiin, called 'The Opal, the Pearl and the Peacock'."

He put the pipe to his lips and began to play, very skillfully indeed, and Ludowik followed him, filling in gaps, making chords. Ameth, forgetting her vexation, listened with eyes half-closed, and moved her arm to the rhythm.

"Did you enjoy that?" asked Guyal, when he had finished.

"Very much. Perhaps you would try it on Uncle Ludowik's flute? It is a fine flute to play, very soft and easy to the breath."

"No," said Guyal, with sudden obstinacy. "I am able to play only my own instrument." He blew again, and it was a dance of the festival, a quirking carnival air. Ludowik, playing with supernal skill, ran merry phrases as might fit, and Ameth, carried away by the rhythm, danced a dance of her own, a merry step in time to the music.

Guyal played a wild tarantella of the peasant folk, and Ameth danced wilder and faster, flung her arms, wheeled, jerked her head in a fine display. And Ludowik's flute played a brilliant obbligato, hurtling over, now under, chording, veering, warping little silver strings of sound around Guyal's melody, adding urgent little grace-phrases.

Ludowik's eyes now clung to the whirling figure of the dancing girl. And suddenly he struck up a theme of his own, a tune of wildest abandon, of a frenzied beating rhythm; and Guyal, carried away by the force of the music, blew as he never had blown before, invented trills and runs, gyrating arpeggios, blew high and shrill, loud and fast and clear.

It was as nothing to Ludowik's music. His eyes were starting; sweat streamed from his seamed old forehead; his flute tore the air into quivering ecstatic shreds.

Ameth danced frenzy; she was no longer beautiful, she appeared grotesque and unfamiliar. The music became something more than the senses could bear. Guyal's own vision turned pink and gray; he saw Ameth fall in a faint, in a foaming fit; and Ludowik, fiery-eyed, staggered erect, hobbled to her body and began a terrible intense concord, slow measures of most solemn and frightening meaning.

Ludowik played death.

Guyal of Sfere turned and ran wide-eyed from the hall. Ludowik, never noticing, continued his terrible piping, played as if every note were a skewer through the twitching girl's shoulder-blades.

Guyal ran through the night, and cold air bit at him like sleet. He burst into the shed, and the white horse softly nickered at him. On with the saddle, on with the bridle, away down the streets of old Carchasel, past the gaping black windows, ringing down the starlit cobbles, away from the music of death!

Guyal of Sfere galloped up the mountain with the stars in his face, and not until he came to the shoulder did he turn in the saddle to look back.

The verging of dawn trembled into the stony valley. Where was Carchasel? There was no city — only a crumble of ruins...

Hark! A far sound?...

No. All was silence.

And yet...

No. Only crumbled stones in the floor of the valley.

Guyal, fixed of eye, turned and went his way, along the trail which stretched north before him.

The walls of the defile which led the trail were steep gray granite, stained scarlet and black by lichen, mildewed blue. The horse's hooves made a hollow clop-clop-clop on the stone, loud to Guyal's ears, hypnotic to his brain, and after the sleepless night he found his frame sagging. His eyes grew dim and warm with drowsiness, but the trail ahead led to unseen vistas, and the void in Guyal's brain drove him without surcease.

The lassitude became such that Guyal slipped halfway from his saddle. Rousing himself, he resolved to round one more bend in the trail and then take rest.

The rock beetled above and hid the sky where the sun had passed the zenith. The trail twisted around a shoulder of rock; ahead shone a patch of indigo heaven. One more turning, Guyal told himself. The defile fell open, the mountains were at his back and he looked out across a hundred miles of steppe. It was a land shaded with subtle colors, washed with delicate shadows, fading and melting into the lurid haze at the horizon. He saw a lone eminence cloaked by a dark company of trees, the glisten of a lake at its foot. To the other side a ranked mass of gray-white ruins was barely discernible. The Museum of Man? ... After a moment of vacillation, Guyal dismounted and sought sleep within the Expansible Egg.

The sun rolled in sad sumptuous majesty behind the mountains; murk fell across the tundra. Guyal awoke and refreshed himself in a rill nearby. Giving meal to his horse, he ate dry fruit and bread; then he mounted and rode down the trail. The plain spread vastly north before him, into desolation; the mountains lowered black above and behind; a slow cold breeze blew in his face. Gloom deepened; the plain sank from sight like a drowned land. Hesitant before the murk, Guyal reined his horse. Better, he thought, to ride in the morning. If he lost the trail in the dark, who could tell what he might encounter?

A mournful sound. Guyal stiffened and turned his face to the sky. A sigh? A moan? A sob? ... Another sound, closer, the rustle of cloth, a loose garment. Guyal cringed into his saddle. Floating slowly down through the darkness came a shape robed in white. Under the cowl and glowing with eer-light looked a drawn face with eyes like the holes in a skull.

It breathed its sad sound and drifted away on high ... There was only the blow of the wind past Guyal's ears.

He drew a shuddering breath and slumped against the pommel. His shoulders felt exposed, naked. He slipped to the ground and established the shelter of the Egg about himself and his horse. Preparing his pallet, he lay himself down; presently, as he lay staring into the dark, sleep came on him and so the night passed.

He awoke before dawn and once more set forth. The trail was a ribbon of white sand between banks of gray furze and the miles passed swiftly.

The trail led toward the tree-clothed eminence Guyal had noted from above; now he thought to see roofs through the heavy foliage and smoke on the sharp air. And presently to right and left spread cultivated fields of spikenard, callow and mead-apple. Guyal continued with eyes watchful for men.

To one side appeared a fence of stone and black timber: the stone chiseled and hewn to the semblance of four globes beaded on a central pillar, the black timbers which served as rails fitted in sockets and carved in precise spirals. Behind this fence a region of bare earth lay churned, pitted, cratered, burnt and wrenched, as if visited at once by fire and the blow of a tremendous hammer. In wondering speculation Guyal gazed and so did not notice the three men who came quietly upon him.

The horse started nervously; Guyal, turning, saw the three. They barred his road and one held the bridle of his horse.

They were tall, well-formed men, wearing tight suits of somber leather bordered with black. Their headgear was heavy maroon cloth crumpled in precise creases, and leather flaps extended horizontally over each ear. Their faces were long and solemn, with clear golden-ivory skin, golden eyes and jet-black hair. Clearly they were not savages: they moved with a silky control, they eyed Guyal with critical appraisal, their garb implied the discipline of an ancient convention.

The leader stepped forward. His expression was neither threat nor welcome. "Greetings, stranger; whither bound?"

"Greetings," replied Guyal cautiously. "I go as my star directs... You are the Saponids?"

"That is our race, and before you is our town Saponce." He inspected Guyal with frank curiosity. "By the color of your custom I suspect your home to be in the south."

"I am Guyal of Sfere, by the River Scaum in Ascolais."

"The way is long," observed the Saponid. "Terrors beset the traveler.

Your impulse must be most intense, and your star must draw with fervent allure."

"I come," said Guyal, "on a pilgrimage for the ease of my spirit; the road seems short when it attains its end."

The Saponid offered polite acquiescence. "Then you have crossed the Fer Aquilas?"

"Indeed; through cold wind and desolate stone." Guyal glanced back at the looming mass. "Only yesterday at night-fall did I leave the gap. And then a ghost hovered above till I thought the grave was marking me for its own."

He paused in surprise; his words seemed to have released a powerful emotion in the Saponids. Their features lengthened, their mouths grew white and clenched. The leader, his polite detachment a trifle diminished, searched the sky with ill-concealed apprehension. "A ghost… In a white garment, thus and so, floating on high?"

"Yes; is it a known familiar of the region?"

There was a pause.

"In a certain sense," said the Saponid. "It is a signal of woe… But I interrupt your tale."

"There is little to tell. I took shelter for the night, and this morning I fared down to the plain."

"Were you not molested further? By Koolbaw the Walking Serpent, who ranges the slopes like fate?"

"I saw neither walking serpent nor crawling lizard; further, a blessing protects my trail and I come to no harm so long as I keep my course."

"Interesting, interesting."

"Now," said Guyal, "permit me to inquire of you, since there is much I would learn; what is this ghost and what evil does he commemorate?"

"You ask beyond my certain knowledge," replied the Saponid cautiously. "Of this ghost it is well not to speak lest our attention reinforce his malignity."

"As you will," replied Guyal. "Perhaps you will instruct me…" He caught his tongue. Before inquiring for the Museum of Man, it would be wise to learn in what regard the Saponids held it, lest, learning his interest, they seek to prevent him from knowledge.

"Yes?" inquired the Saponid. "What is your lack?"

Guyal indicated the seared area behind the fence of stone and timber. "What is the portent of this devastation?"

The Saponid stared across the area with a blank expression and shrugged. "It is one of the ancient places; so much is known, no more. Death lingers here, and no creature may venture across the place without succumbing to a most malicious magic which raises virulence and angry sores. Here is where those whom we kill are sent… But away. You will desire to rest and refresh yourself at Saponce. Come; we will guide you."

He turned down the trail toward the town, and Guyal, finding neither words nor reasons to reject the idea, urged his horse forward.

As they approached the tree-shrouded hill the trail widened to a road. To the right hand the lake drew close, behind low banks of purple reeds. Here were docks built of heavy black baulks and boats rocked to the wind-feathered ripples. They were built in the shape of sickles, with bow and stern curving high from the water.

Up into the town, and the houses were hewn timber, ranging in tone from golden brown to weathered black. The construction was intricate and ornate, the walls rising three stories to steep gables overhanging front and back. Pillars and piers were carved with complex designs: meshing ribbons, tendrils, leaves, lizards, and the like. The screens which guarded the windows were likewise carved, with foliage patterns, animal faces, radiant stars: rich textures in the mellow wood. It was clear that much expressiveness had been expended on the carving.

Up the steep lane, under the gloom cast by the trees, past the houses half-hidden by the foliage, and the Saponids of Saponce came forth to stare. They moved quietly and spoke in low voices, and their garments were of an elegance Guyal had not expected to see on the northern steppe.

His guide halted and turned to Guyal. "Will you oblige me by waiting till I report to the Voyevode, that he may prepare a suitable reception?"

The request was framed in candid words and with guileless eyes. Guyal thought to perceive ambiguity in the phrasing, but since the hooves of his horse were planted in the center of the road, and since he did not propose leaving the road, Guyal assented with an open face.

The Saponid disappeared and Guyal sat musing on the pleasant town perched so high above the plain.

A group of girls approached to glance at Guyal with curious eyes. Guyal returned the inspection, and now found a puzzling lack about their persons, a discrepancy which he could not instantly identify. They wore graceful garments of woven wool, striped and dyed various colors; they were supple and slender, and seemed not lacking in coquetry. And yet…

The Saponid returned. "Now, Sir Guyal, may we proceed?"

Guyal, endeavoring to remove any flavor of suspicion from his words, said, "You will understand, Sir Saponid, that by the very nature of my father's blessing I dare not leave the delineated course of the trail; for then, instantly, I would become liable to any curse, which, placed on me along the way, might be seeking just such occasion for leeching close on my soul."

The Saponid made an understanding gesture. "Naturally; you follow a sound principle. Let me reassure you. I but conduct you to a reception by the Voyevode who even now hastens to the plaza to greet a stranger from the far south."

Guyal bowed in gratification, and they continued up the road.

A hundred paces and the road levelled, crossing a common planted with small, fluttering, heart shaped leaves, colored in all shades of purple, red, green and black.

The Saponid turned to Guyal. "As a stranger I must caution you never to set foot on the common. It is one of our sacred places, and tradition requires that a severe penalty be exacted for transgressions and sacrilege."

"I note your warning," said Guyal. "I will respectfully obey your law."

They passed a dense thicket; with hideous clamor a bestial shape sprang from concealment, a creature staring-eyed with tremendous fanged jaws. Guyal's horse shied, bolted, sprang out on to the sacred common and trampled the fluttering leaves.

A number of Saponid men rushed forth, grasped the horse, seized Guyal and dragged him from the saddle.

"Ho!" cried Guyal. "What means this? Release me!"

The Saponid who had been his guide advanced, shaking his head in reproach. "Indeed, and only had I just impressed upon you the gravity of such an offense!"

"But the monster frightened my horse!" said Guyal. "I am no wise responsible for this trespass; release me, let us proceed to the reception."

The Saponid said, "I fear that the penalties prescribed by tradition must come into effect. Your protests, though of superficial plausibility, will not bear serious examination. For instance, the creature you term a monster is in reality a harmless domesticated beast. Secondly, I observe the animal you bestride; he will not make a turn or twist without the twitch of the reins. Thirdly, even if your postulates were conceded, you thereby admit to guilt by virtue of negligence and omission. You should have secured a mount less apt to unpredictable action, or upon learning of the sanctitude of the common, you should have considered such a contingency as even now occurred, and therefore dismounted, leading your beast. Therefore, Sir Guyal, though loath, I am forced to believe you guilty of impertinence, impiety, disregard and impudicity. Therefore, as Castellan and Sergeant-Reader of the Litany, so responsible for the detention of law-breakers, I must order you secured, contained, pent, incarcerated and confined until such time as the penalties will be exacted."

"The entire episode is mockery!" raged Guyal. "Are you savages, then, thus to mistreat a lone wayfarer?"

"By no means," replied the Castellan. "We are a highly civilized people, with customs bequeathed us by the past. Since the past was more glorious than the present, what presumption we would show by questioning these laws!"

Guyal fell quiet. "And what are the usual penalties for my act?"

The Castellan made a reassuring motion. "The rote prescribes three acts of penance, which in your case, I am sure will be nominal. But— the forms must be observed, and it is necessary that you be constrained in the Felon's Caseboard." He motioned to the men who held Guyal's arm. "Away with him; cross neither track nor trail, for then your grasp will be nerveless and he will be delivered from justice."

Guyal was pent in a well-aired but poorly lighted cellar of stone. The floor he found dry, the ceiling free of crawling insects. He had not been searched, nor had his Scintillant Dagger been removed from his sash.

With suspicions crowding his brain he lay on the rush bed and, after a period, slept.

Now ensued the passing of a day. He was given food and drink; and at last the Castellan came to visit him.

"You are indeed fortunate," said the Saponid, "in that, as a witness, I was able to suggest your delinquencies to be more the result of negligence than malice. The last penalties exacted for the crime were stringent; the felon was ordered to perform the following three acts: first, to cut off his toes and sew the severed members into the skin at his neck; second, to revile his forbears for three hours, commencing with a Common Bill of Anathema, including feigned madness and hereditary disease, and at last defiling the hearth of his clan with ordure; and third, walking a mile under the lake with leaded shoes in search of the Lost Book of Qualls." And the Castellan regarded Guyal with complacency.

"What deeds must I perform?" inquired Guyal drily.

The Castellan joined the tips of his fingers together. "As I say, the penances are nominal, by decree of the Voyevode. First you must swear never again to repeat your crime."

"That I gladly do," said Guyal, and so bound himself.

"Second," said the Castellan with a slight smile, "you must adjudicate at a Grand Pageant of Pulchritude among the maids of the village and select her whom you deem the most beautiful."

"Scarcely an arduous task," commented Guyal. "Why does it fall to my lot?"

The Castellan looked vaguely to the ceiling. "There are a number of concomitants to victory in this contest... Every person in the town would find relations among the participants — a daughter, a sister, a niece — and so would hardly be considered unprejudiced. The charge of favoritism could never be levelled against you; therefore you make an ideal selection for this important post."

Guyal seemed to hear the ring of sincerity in the Saponid's voice; still he wondered why the selection of the town's loveliest was a matter of such import.

"And third?" he inquired.

"That will be revealed after the contest, which occurs this afternoon."

The Saponid departed the cell.

Guyal, who was not without vanity, spent several hours restoring himself and his costume from the ravages of travel. He bathed, trimmed his hair, shaved his face, and, when the Castellan came to unlock the door, he felt that he made no discreditable picture.

He was led out upon the road and directed up the hill toward the summit of the terraced town of Saponce. Turning to the Castellan he said, "How is it that you permit me to walk the trail once more? You must know that now I am safe from molestation..."

The Castellan shrugged. "True. But you would gain little by insisting upon your temporary immunity. Ahead the trail crosses a bridge, which we could demolish; behind we need but breach the dam to Peilvemchal Torrent; then, should you walk the trail, you would be swept to the side and so rendered vulnerable. No, Sir Guyal of Sfere, once the secret of your immunity is abroad then you are liable to a variety of stratagems. For instance, a large wall might be placed athwart the way, before and behind you. No doubt the spell would preserve you from thirst and hunger, but what then? So would you sit till the sun went out."

Guyal said no word. Across the lake he noticed a trio of the crescent boats approaching the docks, prows and sterns rocking and dipping into the shaded water with a graceful motion. The void in his mind made itself known. "Why are boats constructed in such fashion?"

The Castellan looked blankly at him. "It is the only practicable method. Do not the oe-pods grow thusly to the south?"

"Never have I seen oe-pods."

"They are the fruit of a great vine, and grow in scimitar-shape. When sufficiently large, we cut and clean them, slit the inner edge, grapple end to end with strong line and constrict till the pod opens as is desirable. Then when cured, dried, varnished, carved, burnished, and lacquered; fitted with deck, thwarts and gussets — then have we our boats."

They entered the plaza, a flat area at the summit surrounded on three sides by tall houses of carved dark wood. The fourth side was open to a vista across the lake and beyond to the loom of the mountains. Trees overhung all and the sun shining through made a scarlet pattern on the sandy floor.

To Guyal's surprise there seemed to be no preliminary ceremonies or formalities to the contest, and small spirit of festivity was manifest among the townspeople. Indeed they seemed beset by subdued despondency and eyed him without enthusiasm.

A hundred girls stood gathered in a disconsolate group in the center of the plaza. It seemed to Guyal that they had gone to few pains to embellish themselves for beauty. To the contrary, they wore shapeless rags, their hair seemed deliberately misarranged, their faces dirty and scowling.

Guyal stared and turned to his guide. "These girls seem not to relish the garland of pulchritude."

The Castellan nodded wryly. "As you see, they are by no means jealous for distinction; modesty has always been a Saponid trait."

Guyal hesitated. "What is the form of procedure? I do not desire in my ignorance to violate another of your arcane apochrypha."

The Castellan said with a blank face, "There are no formalities. We conduct these pageants with expedition and the least possible ceremony. You need but pass among these maidens and point out her whom you deem the most attractive."

Guyal advanced to his task, feeling more than half-foolish. Then he reflected: this is a penalty for contravening an absurd tradition; I will conduct myself with efficiency and so the quicker rid myself of the obligation.

He stood before the hundred girls, who eyed him with hostility and anxiety, and Guyal saw that his task would not be simple, since, on the whole, they were of a comeliness which even the dirt, grimacing and rags could not disguise.

"Range yourselves, if you please, into a line," said Guyal. "In this way, none will be at disadvantage."

Sullenly the girls formed a line.

Guyal surveyed the group. He saw at once that a number could be eliminated: the squat, the obese, the lean, the pocked and coarse-featured — perhaps a quarter of the group. He said suavely, "Never have I seen such unanimous loveliness; each of you might legitimately claim the cordon. My task is arduous; I must weigh fine imponderables; in the end my choice will undoubtedly be based on subjectivity and those of real charm will no doubt be the first discharged from the competition." He stepped forward. "Those whom I indicate may retire."

He walked down the line, pointing, and the ugliest, with expressions of unmistakable relief, hastened to the sidelines.

A second time Guyal made his inspection, and now, somewhat more familiar with those he judged, he was able to discharge those who, while suffering no whit from ugliness, were merely plain.

Roughly a third of the original group remained. These stared at Guyal with varying degrees of apprehension and truculence as he passed before them, studying each in turn... All at once his mind was determined, and his choice definite. Somehow the girls felt the change in him, and in their anxiety and tension left off the expressions they had been wearing to daunt and bemuse him.

Guyal made one last survey down the line. No, he had been accurate in his choice. There were girls here as comely as the senses could desire, girls with opal-glowing eyes and hyacinth features, girls as lissome as reeds, with hair silky and fine despite the dust which they seemed to have rubbed upon themselves.

The girl whom Guyal had selected was slighter than the others and possessed of a beauty not at once obvious. She had a small triangular face, great wistful eyes and thick black hair cut raggedly short at the ears. Her skin was of a transparent paleness, like the finest ivory; her form slender, graceful, and of a compelling magnetism, urgent of intimacy. She seemed to have sensed his decision and her eyes widened.

Guyal took her hand, led her forward, and turned to the Voyevode — an old man sitting stolidly in a heavy chair.

"This is she whom I find the loveliest among your maidens."

There was silence through the square. Then there came a hoarse sound, a cry of sadness from the Castellan and Sergeant-Reader. He came forward, sagging of face, limp of body. "Guyal of Sfere, you have wrought a great revenge for my tricking you. This is my beloved daughter, Shierl, whom you have designated for dread."

Guyal turned in wonderment from the Castellan to the girl Shierl, in whose eyes he now recognized a film of numbness, a gazing into a great depth.

Returning to the Castellan, Guyal stammered, "I meant but complete impersonality. This your daughter Shierl I find one of the loveliest creatures of my experience; I cannot understand where I have offended."

"No, Guyal," said the Castellan, "you have chosen fairly, for such indeed is my own thought."

"Well then," said Guyal, "reveal to me now my third task that I may have done and continue my pilgrimage."

The Castellan said, "Three leagues to the north lies the ruin which tradition tells us to be the olden Museum of Man."

"Ah," said Guyal, "go on, I attend."

"You must, as your third charge, conduct this my daughter Shierl to the Museum of Man. At the portal you will strike on a copper gong and announce to whomever responds: 'We are those summoned from Saponce.'"

Guyal started, frowned. "How is this? 'We'?"

"Such is your charge," said the Castellan in a voice like thunder.

Guyal looked to left, right, forward and behind. But he stood in the center of the plaza surrounded by the hardy men of Saponce.

"When must this charge be executed?" he inquired in a controlled voice.

The Castellan said in a voice bitter as oak-wort: "Even now Shierl goes to clothe herself in yellow. In one hour shall she appear, in one hour shall you set forth for the Museum of Man."

"And then?"

"And then — for good or for evil, it is not known. You fare as thirteen thousand have fared before you."

Down from the plaza, down the leafy lanes of Saponce came Guyal, indignant and clamped of mouth, though the pit of his stomach felt tender and heavy with trepidation. The ritual carried distasteful overtones: execution or sacrifice. Guyal's step faltered.

The Castellan seized his elbow with a hard hand. "Forward."

Execution or sacrifice…The faces along the lane swam with morbid curiosity, inner excitement; gloating eyes searched him deep to relish his fear and horror, and the mouths half-drooped, half-smiled in the inner hugging for joy not to be the one walking down the foliage streets, and forth to the Museum of Man.

The eminence, with the tall trees and carved dark houses, was at his back; they walked out into the claret sunlight of the tundra. Here were eighty women in white chlamys with ceremonial buckets of woven straw over their heads; around a tall tent of yellow silk they stood.

The Castellan halted Guyal and beckoned to the Ritual Matron. She flung back the hangings at the door of the tent; the girl within, Shierl, came slowly forth, eyes wide and dark with fright.

She wore a stiff gown of yellow brocade, and the wand of her body seemed pent and constrained within. The gown came snug under her chin, left her arms bare and raised past the back of her head in a stiff spear-headed cowl. She was frightened as a small animal trapped is frightened; she stared at Guyal, at her father, as if she had never seen them before.

The Ritual Matron put a gentle hand on her waist, propelled her forward. Shierl stepped once, twice, irresolutely halted. The Castellan brought Guyal forward and placed him at the girl's side; now two children, a boy and a girl, came hastening up with cups which they proffered to Guyal and Shierl. Dully she accepted the cup. Guyal took his and glanced suspiciously at the murky brew. He looked up to the Castellan. "What is the nature of this potion?"

"Drink," said the Castellan. "So will your way seem the shorter; so will terror leave you behind, and you will march to the Museum with a steadier step."

"No," said Guyal. "I will not drink. My senses must be my own when I meet the Curator. I have come far for the privilege; I would not stultify the occasion stumbling and staggering." And he handed the cup back to the boy.

Shierl stared dully at the cup she held. Said Guyal: "I advise you likewise to avoid the drug; so will we come to the Museum of Man with our dignity to us."

Hesitantly she returned the cup. The Castellan's brow clouded, but he made no protest.

An old man in a black costume brought forward a satin pillow on which rested a whip with a handle of carved steel. The Castellan now lifted this whip, and advancing, laid three light strokes across the shoulders of both Shierl and Guyal.

"Now, I charge thee, get hence and go from Saponce, outlawed forever; thou art waifs forlorn. Seek succor at the Museum of Man. I charge thee, never look back, leave all thoughts of past and future here at North Garden. Now and forever are you sundered from all bonds, claims, relations, and kinships, together with all pretenses to amity, love, fellowship and brotherhood with the Saponids of Saponce. Go, I exhort; go, I command; go, go, go!"

Shierl sunk her teeth into her lower lip; tears freely coursed her cheek though she made no sound. With hanging head she started across the lichen of the tundra, and Guyal, with a swift stride, joined her.

Now there was no looking back. For a space the murmurs, the nervous sounds followed their ears; then they were alone on the plain. The limitless north lay across the horizon; the tundra filled the foreground and background, an expanse dreary, dun and moribund. Alone marring the region, the white ruins — once the Museum of Man — rose a league before them, and along the faint trail they walked without words.

Guyal said in a tentative tone, "There is much I would understand."

"Speak," said Shierl. Her voice was low but composed.

"Why are we forced and exhorted to this mission?"

"It is thus because it has always been thus. Is not this reason enough?"

"Sufficient possibly for you," said Guyal, "but for me the causality is unconvincing. I must acquaint you with the void in my mind, which lusts for knowledge as a lecher yearns for carnality; so pray be patient if my inquisition seems unnecessarily thorough."

She glanced at him in astonishment. "Are all to the south so strong for knowing as you?"

"In no degree," said Guyal. "Everywhere normality of the mind may be observed. The habitants adroitly perform the motions which fed them yesterday, last week, a year ago. I have been informed of my aberration well and full. 'Why strive for a pedant's accumulation?' I have been told. 'Why forego merriment, music, and revelry for the abstract and abstruse?' "

"Indeed," said Shierl. "Well do they counsel; such is the consensus at Saponce."

Guyal shrugged. "The rumor goes that I am demon-bereft of my senses. Such may be. In any event the effect remains and the obsession haunts me."

Shierl indicated understanding and acquiescence. "Ask on then; I will endeavor to ease these yearnings."

He glanced at her sidelong, studied the charming triangle of her face, the heavy black hair, the great lustrous eyes, dark as yu-sapphires. "In happier circumstances, there would be other yearnings I would beseech you likewise to ease."

"Ask," replied Shierl of Saponce. "The Museum of Man is close; there is occasion for naught but words."

"Why are we thus dismissed and charged, with tacit acceptance of our doom?"

"The immediate cause is the ghost you saw on the hill. When the ghost appears, then we of Saponce know that the most beautiful maiden and the most handsome youth of the town must be despatched to the Museum. The prime behind the custom I do not know. So it is; so it has been; so it will be till the sun gutters like a coal in the rain and darkens Earth, and the winds blow snow over Saponce."

"But what is our mission? Who greets us, what is our fate?"

"Such details are unknown."

Guyal mused, "The likelihood of pleasure seems small... There are discordants in the episode. You are beyond doubt the loveliest creature of the Saponids, the loveliest creature of Earth—but I, I am a casual stranger, and hardly the most well-favored youth of the town."

She smiled a trifle. "You are not uncomely."

Guyal said somberly, "Over-riding the condition of my person is the fact that I am a stranger and so bring little loss to the town of Saponce."

"That aspect has no doubt been considered," the girl said.

Guyal searched the horizon. "Let us then avoid the Museum of Man, let us circumvent this unknown fate and take to the mountains, and so south to Ascolais. Lust for enlightenment will never fly me in the face of destruction so clearly implicit."

She shook her head. "Do you suppose that we would gain by the ruse? The eyes of a hundred warriors follow us till we pass through the portals of the Museum; should we attempt to scamp our duty we should be bound to stakes, stripped of our skins by the inch, and at last be placed in bags with a thousand scorpions poured around our heads. Such is the traditional penalty; twelve times in history has it been invoked."

Guyal threw back his shoulders and spoke in a nervous voice. "Ah, well — the Museum of Man has been my goal for many years. On this motive I set forth from Sfere, so now I would seek the Curator and satisfy my obsession for brainfilling."

"You are blessed with great fortune," said Shierl, "for you are being granted your heart's desire."

Guyal could find nothing to say, so for a space they walked in silence. Then he spoke. "Shierl."

"Yes, Guyal of Sfere?"

"Do they separate us and take us apart?"

"I do not know."

"Shierl."

"Yes?"

"Had we met under a happier star…" He paused.

Shierl walked in silence.

He looked at her coolly. "You speak not."

"But you ask nothing," she said in surprise. Guyal turned his face ahead, to the Museum of Man.

Presently she touched his arm. "Guyal, I am greatly frightened."

Guyal gazed at the ground beneath his feet, and a blossom of fire sprang alive in his brain. "See the marking through the lichen?"

"Yes; what then?"

"Is it a trail?"

Dubiously she responded, "It is a way worn by the passage of many feet. So then — it is a trail."

Guyal said in restrained jubilation, "Here is safety, if I never permit myself to be cozened from the way. But you — ah, I must guard you; you must never leave my side, you must swim in the charm which protects me; perhaps then we will survive."

Shierl said sadly, "Let us not delude our reason, Guyal of Sfere."

But as they walked, the trail grew plainer, and Guyal became correspondingly sanguine. And ever larger bulked the crumble which marked the Museum of Man, presently to occupy all their vision.

If a storehouse of knowledge had existed here, little sign of it remained. There was a great flat floor, flagged in white stone, now chalky, broken and inter-thrust by weeds. Around this floor rose a series of monoliths, pocked and worn, and toppled off at various heights. These at one time had supported a vast roof; now of roof there was none and the walls were but dreams of the far past.

So here was the flat floor bounded by the broken stumps of pillars, bare to the winds of time and the glare of cool red sun. The rains had washed the marble, the dust from the mountains had been laid on and swept off, laid on and swept off, and those who had built the Museum were less than a mote of this dust, so far and forgotten were they.

"Think," said Guyal, "think of the vastness of knowledge which once was gathered here and which is now one with the soil — unless, of course, the Curator has salvaged and preserved."

Shierl looked about apprehensively. "I think rather of the portal, and that which awaits us... Guyal," she whispered, "I fear, I fear greatly... Suppose they tear us apart? Suppose there is torture and death for us? I fear a tremendous impingement, the shock of horror..."

Guyal's own throat was hot and full. He looked about with challenge. "While I still breathe and hold power in my arms to fight, there will be none to harm us."

Shierl groaned softly. "Guyal, Guyal, Guyal of Sfere — why did you choose me?"

"Because," said Guyal, "my eye went to you like the nectar moth flits to the jacynth; because you were the loveliest and I thought nothing but good in store for you."

With a shuddering breath Shierl said, "I must be courageous; after all, if it were not I it would be some other maid equally fearful... And there is the portal."

Guyal inhaled deeply, inclined his head, and strode forward. "Let us be to it, and know..."

The portal opened into a nearby monolith, a door of flat black metal. Guyal followed the trail to the door, and rapped staunchly with his fist on the small copper gong to the side.

The door groaned wide on its hinges, and cool air, smelling of the under-earth, billowed forth. In the black gape their eyes could find nothing.

"Hola within!" cried Guyal.

A soft voice, full of catches and quavers, as if just after weeping, said, "Come ye, come ye forward. You are desired and awaited."

Guyal leaned his head forward, straining to see. "Give us light, that we may not wander from the trail and bottom ourselves."

The breathless quaver of a voice said, "Light is not needed; anywhere you step, that will be your trail, by an arrangement so agreed with the Way-Maker."

"No," said Guyal, "we would see the visage of our host. We come at his invitation; the minimum of his guest-offering is light; light there must be before we set foot inside the dungeon. Know we come as seekers after knowledge; we are visitors to be honored."

"Ah, knowledge, knowledge," came the sad breathlessness. "That shall be yours, in full plentitude — knowledge of many strange affairs; oh, you shall swim in a tide of knowledge —"

Guyal interrupted the sad, sighing voice. "Are you the Curator? Hundreds of leagues have I come to bespeak the Curator and put him my inquiries. Are you he?"

"By no means. I revile the name of the Curator as a treacherous non-essential."

"Who then may you be?"

"I am no one, nothing. I am an abstraction, an emotion, the ooze of terror, the sweat of horror, the shake in the air when a scream has departed."

"You speak the voice of man."

"Why not? Such things as I speak lie in the closest and dearest center of the human brain."

Guyal said in a subdued voice, "You do not make your invitation as enticing as might be hoped."

"No matter, no matter; enter you must, into the dark and on the instant, as my lord, who is myself, waxes warm and languorous."

"If light there be, we enter."

"No light, no insolent scorch is ever found in the Museum."

"In this case," said Guyal, drawing forth his Scintillant Dagger, "I innovate a welcome reform. For see, now there is light!"

From the under-pommel issued a searching glare; the ghost tall before them screeched and fell into twinkling ribbons like pulverized tinsel. There were a few vagrant motes in the air; he was gone.

Shierl, who had stood stark and stiff as one mesmerized, gasped a soft warm gasp and fell against Guyal. "How can you be so defiant?"

Guyal said in a voice half-laugh, half-quaver, "In truth I do not know... perhaps I find it incredible that Destiny would direct me from pleasant Sfere, through forest and crag, into the northern waste, merely to play the role of cringing victim. Disbelieving so inconclusive a destiny, I am bold."

He moved the dagger to right and left, and they saw themselves to be at the portal of a keep, cut from concreted rock. At the back opened a black depth. Crossing the floor swiftly, Guyal kneeled and listened.

He heard no sound. Shierl, at his back, stared with eyes as black and deep as the pit itself, and Guyal, turning, received a sudden irrational impression of a sprite of the olden times — a creature small and delicate, heavy with the weight of her charm, pale, sweet, clean.

Leaning with his glowing dagger, he saw a crazy rack of stairs voyaging down into the dark, and his light showed them and their shadows in so confusing a guise that he blinked and drew back.

Shierl said, "What do you fear?"

Guyal rose, turned to her. "We are momentarily untended here in the Museum of Man, and we are impelled forward by various forces; you by the will of your people; I, by that which has driven me since I first tasted air... If we stay here we shall be once more arranged in harmony with the hostile pattern. If we go forward boldly, we may so come to a position of strategy and advantage. I propose that we set forth in all courage, descend these stairs and seek the Curator."

"But does he exist?"

"The ghost spoke fervently against him."

"Let us go then," said Shierl. "I am resigned."

Guyal said gravely, "We go in the mental frame of adventure, aggressiveness, zeal. Thus does fear vanish and the ghosts become creatures of mind-weft; thus does our élan burst the under-earth terror."

"We go."

They started down the stairs.

Back, forth, back, forth, down flights at varying angles, stages of varying heights, treads at varying widths, so that each step was a matter for concentration. Back, forth, down, down, down, and the black-barred shadows moved and jerked in bizarre modes on the walls.

The flight ended, they stood in a room similar to the entry above. Before them was another black portal, polished at one spot by use; on the walls to either side were inset brass plaques bearing messages in unfamiliar characters.

Guyal pushed the door open against a slight pressure of cold air, which, blowing through the aperture, made a slight rush, ceasing when Guyal opened the door farther.

"Listen."

It was a far sound, an intermittent clacking, and it held enough fell significance to raise the hairs at Guyal's neck. He felt Shierl's hand gripping his with clammy pressure.

Dimming the dagger's glow to a glimmer, Guyal passed through the door, with Shierl coming after. From afar came the evil sound, and by the echoes they knew they stood in a great hall.

Guyal directed the light to the floor: it was of a black resilient material. Next the wall: polished stone. He permitted the light to glow in the direction opposite to the sound, and a few paces distant they saw a bulky black case, studded with copper bosses, topped by a shallow glass tray in which could be seen an intricate concourse of metal devices.

With the purpose of the black cases not apparent, they followed the wall, and as they walked similar cases appeared, looming heavy and dull, at regular intervals. The clacking receded as they walked; then they came to a right angle, and turning the corner, they seemed to approach the sound. Black case after black case passed; slowly, tense as foxes, they walked, eyes groping for sight through the darkness.

The wall made another angle, and here there was a door.

Guyal hesitated. To follow the new direction of the wall would mean approaching the source of the sound. Would it be better to discover the worst quickly or to reconnoitre as they went?

He propounded the dilemma to Shierl, who shrugged. "It is all one; sooner or later the ghosts will flit down to pluck at us; then we are lost."

"Not while I possess light to stare them away to wisps and shreds," said Guyal. "Now I would find the Curator, and possibly he is to be found behind this door. We will so discover."

He laid his shoulder to the door; it eased ajar with a crack of golden light. Guyal peered through. He sighed, a muffled sound of wonder.

Now he opened the door further; Shierl clutched at his arm.

"This is the Museum," said Guyal in rapt tone. "Here there is no danger... He who dwells in beauty of this sort may never be other than beneficent..." He flung wide the door.

The light came from an unknown source, from the air itself, as if leaking from the discrete atoms; every breath was luminous, the room floated full of invigorating glow. A great rug pelted the floor, a monster tabard woven of gold, brown, bronze, two tones of green, fuscous red and smalt blue. Beautiful works of human fashioning ranked the walls. In glorious array hung panels of rich woods, carved, chased, enameled; scenes of olden times painted on woven fiber; formulas of color, designed to convey emotion rather than reality. To one side hung plats of wood laid on with slabs of soapstone, malachite and jade in rectangular patterns, richly varied and subtle, with miniature flecks of cinnabar, rhodochrosite and coral for warmth. Beside was a section given to disks of luminous green, flickering and fluorescent with varying blue films and moving dots of scarlet and black. Here were representations of three hundred marvellous flowers, blooms of a forgotten age, no longer extant on waning Earth; there were as many starburst patterns, rigidly conventionalized in form, but each of subtle distinction. All these and a multitude of other creations, selected from the best of human fervor.

The door thudded softly behind them; staring, every inch of skin a-tingle, the two from Earth's final time moved forward through the hall.

"Somewhere near must be the Curator," whispered Guyal. "There is a sense of careful tending and great effort here in the gallery."

"Look."

Opposite were two doors, laden with the sense of much use. Guyal strode quickly across the room but was unable to discern the means for opening the door, for it bore no latch, key, handle, knob or bar. He rapped with his knuckles and waited; no sound returned.

Shierl tugged at his arm. "These are private regions. It is best not to venture too rudely."

Guyal turned away and they continued down the gallery. Past the real expression of man's brightest dreamings they walked, until the concentration of so much fire and spirit and creativity put them into awe. "What great minds lie in the dust," said Guyal in a low voice. "What gorgeous souls have vanished into the buried ages; what marvellous creatures are lost past the remotest memory... Nevermore will there be the like; now in the last fleeting moments, humanity festers rich as rotten fruit. Rather than master and overpower our world, our highest aim is to cheat it through sorcery."

Shierl said, "But you, Guyal — you are apart. You are not like this..."

"I would know," declared Guyal with fierce emphasis. "In all my youth this ache has driven me, and I have journeyed from the old manse at Sfere to learn from the Curator... I am dissatisfied with the mindless accomplishments of the magicians, who have all their lore by rote."

Shierl gazed at him with a marvelling expression, and Guyal's soul throbbed with love. She felt him quiver and whispered recklessly, "Guyal of Sfere, I am yours, I melt for you..."

"When we win to peace," said Guyal, "then our world will be of gladness..."

The room turned a corner, widened. And now the clacking sound they had noticed in the dark outer hall returned, louder, more suggestive of unpleasantness. It seemed to enter the gallery through an arched doorway opposite.

Guyal moved quietly to this door, with Shierl at his heels, and so they peered into the next chamber.

A great face looked from the wall, a face taller than Guyal, as tall as Guyal might reach with hands on high. The chin rested on the floor, the scalp slanted back into the panel.

Guyal stared, taken aback. In this pageant of beautiful objects, the grotesque visage was the disparity and dissonance a lunatic might have created. Ugly and vile was the face, of a gut-wrenching silly obscenity. The skin shone a gun-metal sheen, the eyes gazed dully from slanting folds of greenish tissue. The nose was a small lump, the mouth a gross pulpy slash.

In sudden uncertainty Guyal turned to Shierl. "Does this not seem an odd work so to be honored here in the Museum of Man?"

Shierl was staring with eyes agonized and wide. Her mouth opened, quivered, wetness streaked her chin. With hands jerking, shaking, she grabbed his arm, staggered back into the gallery.

"Guyal," she cried, "Guyal, come away!" Her voice rose to a pitch. "Come away, come away!"

He faced her in surprise. "What are you saying?"

"That horrible thing in there —"

"It is but the diseased effort of an elder artist."

"It lives."

"How is this!"

"It lives!" she babbled. "It looked at me, then turned and looked at you. And it moved — and then I pulled you away..."

Guyal shrugged off her hand; in stark disbelief he faced through the doorway.

"Ahhhh..." breathed Guyal.

The face had changed. The torpor had evaporated; the glaze had departed the eyes. The mouth squirmed; a hiss of escaping gas sounded. The mouth opened; a great gray tongue lolled forth. And from this tongue darted a tendril slimed with mucus. It terminated in a grasping hand, which groped for Guyal's ankle. He jumped aside; the hand missed its clutch, the tendril coiled.

Guyal, in an extremity, with his bowels clenched by sick fear, sprang back into the gallery. The hand seized Shierl, grasped her ankle. The eyes glistened; and now the flabby tongue swelled another wen, sprouted a new member... Shierl stumbled, fell limp, her eyes staring, foam at her lips. Guyal, shouting in a voice he could not hear, shouting high and crazy, ran forward slashing with his dagger. He cut at the gray wrist, but his knife sprang away as if the steel itself were horrified. His gorge at his teeth, he seized the tendril; with a mighty effort he broke it against his knee.

The face winced, the tendril jerked back. Guyal leapt forward, dragged Shierl into the gallery, lifted her, carried her back, out of reach.

Through the doorway now, Guyal glared in hate and fear. The mouth had closed; it sneered disappointment and frustrated lust. And now Guyal saw a strange thing: from the dank nostril oozed a wisp of white which swirled, writhed, formed a tall thing in a white robe — a thing with a drawn face and eyes like holes in a skull. Whimpering and mewing in distaste for the light, it wavered forward into the gallery, moving with curious little pauses and hesitancies.

Guyal stood still. Fear had exceeded its power; fear no longer had meaning. A brain could react only to the maximum of its intensity; how could this thing harm him now? He would smash it with his hands, beat it into sighing fog.

"Hold, hold, hold!" came a new voice. "Hold, hold, hold. My charms and tokens, an ill day for Thorsingol… But then, avaunt, you ghost, back to the orifice, back and avaunt, avaunt, I say! Go, else I loose the actinics; trespass is not allowed, by supreme command from the Lycurgat; aye, the Lycurgat of Thorsingol. Avaunt, so then."

The ghost wavered, paused, staring in fell passivity at the old man who had hobbled into the gallery.

Back to the snoring face wandered the ghost, and let itself be sucked up into the nostril.

The face rumbled behind its lips, then opened the great gray gape and belched a white fiery lick that was like flame but not flame. It sheeted, flapped at the old man, who moved not an inch. From a rod fixed high on the door frame came a whirling disk of golden sparks. It cut and dismembered the white sheet, destroyed it back to the mouth of the face, whence now issued a black bar. This bar edged into the whirling disk and absorbed the sparks. There was an instant of dead silence.

Then the old man crowed, "Ah, you evil episode; you seek to interrupt my tenure. But no, there is no validity in your purpose; my clever baton holds your unnatural sorcery in abeyance; you are as naught; why do you not disengage and retreat into Jeldred?"

The rumble behind the large lips continued. The mouth opened wide: a gray viscous cavern was so displayed. The eyes glittered in titanic emotion. The mouth yelled, a roaring wave of violence, a sound to buffet the head and drive shock like a nail into the mind.

The baton sprayed a mist of silver. The sound curved and centralized and sucked into the metal fog; the sound was captured and consumed; it was never heard. The fog balled, lengthened to an arrow, plunged with intense speed at the nose, and buried itself in the pulp. There was a heavy sound, an explosion; the face seethed in pain and the nose was a blasted clutter of shredded gray plasms. They waved like starfish arms and grew together once more, and now the nose was pointed like a cone.

The old man said, "You are captious today, my demoniac visitant — a vicious trait. You would disturb poor old Kerlin in his duties? So. You are ingenuous and neglectful. So ho. Baton," and he turned and peered at the rod, "you have tasted that sound? Spew out a fitting penalty, smear the odious face with your infallible retort."

A flat sound, a black flail which curled, slapped the air and smote home to the face. A glowing weal sprang into being. The face sighed and the eyes twisted up into their folds of greenish tissue.

Kerlin the Curator laughed, a shrill yammer on a single tone. He stopped short and the laugh vanished as if it had never begun. He turned to Guyal and Shierl, who stood pressed together in the doorframe.

"How now, how now? You are after the gong; the study hours are long ended. Why do you linger?" He shook a stern finger. "The Museum is not the site for roguery; this I admonish. So now be off, home to Thorsingol; be more prompt the next time; you disturb the established order..." He paused and threw a fretful glance over his shoulder. "The day has gone ill; the Nocturnal Key-keeper is inexcusably late... Surely I have waited an hour on the sluggard; the Lycurgat shall be so informed. I would be home to couch and hearth; here is ill use for old Kerlin, thus to detain him for the careless retard of the night-watch... And, further, the encroachment of you two laggards; away now, and be off; out into the twilight!" And he advanced, making directive motions with his hands.

Guyal said, "My lord Curator, I must speak words with you."

The old man halted, peered. "Eh? What now? At the end of a long day's effort? No, no, you are out of order; regulation must be observed. Attend my audiarium at the fourth circuit tomorrow morning; then we shall hear you. So go now, go."

Guyal fell back nonplussed. Shierl fell on her knees. "Sir Curator, we beg you for help; we have no place to go."

Kerlin the Curator looked at her blankly. "No place to go! What folly you utter! Go to your domicile, or to the Pubescentarium, or to the Temple, or to the Outward Inn. Forsooth, Thorsingol is free with lodging; the Museum is no casual tavern."

"My lord," cried Guyal desperately, "will you hear me? We speak from emergency."

"Say on then."

"Some malignancy has bewitched your brain. Will you credit this?"

"Ah, indeed?" ruminated the Curator.

"There is no Thorsingol. There is naught but dark waste. Your city is an eon gone."

The Curator smiled benevolently. "Ah, sad… A sad case. So it is with these younger minds. The frantic drive of life is the Prime Unhinger." He shook his head. "My duty is clear. Tired bones, you must wait your well-deserved rest. Fatigue — begone; duty and simple humanity make demands; here is madness to be countered and cleared. And in any event the Nocturnal Key-keeper is not here to relieve me of my tedium." He beckoned. "Come."

Hesitantly Guyal and Shierl followed him. He opened one of his doors, passed through muttering and expostulating with doubt and watchfulness. Guyal and Shierl came after.

The room was cubical, floored with dull black stuff, walled with myriad golden knobs on all sides. A hooded chair occupied the center of the room, and beside it was a chest-high lectern whose face displayed a number of toggles and knurled wheels.

"This is the Curator's own Chair of Knowledge," explained Kerlin. "As such it will, upon proper adjustment, impose the Pattern of Hynomeneural Clarity. So — I demand the correct sometsyndic arrangement —" he manipulated the manuals "— and now, if you will compose yourself, I will repair your hallucination. It is beyond my normal call of duty, but I am humane and would not be spoken of as mean or unwilling."

Guyal inquired anxiously, "Lord Curator, this Chair of Clarity, how will it affect me?"

Kerlin the Curator said grandly, "The fibers of your brain are twisted, snarled, frayed, and so make contact with unintentional areas. By the marvellous craft of our modern cerebrologists, this hood will compose your synapses with the correct readings from the library — those of normality, you must understand — and so repair the skein, and make you once more a whole man."

"Once I sit in the chair," Guyal inquired, "what will you do?"

"Merely close this contact, engage this arm, throw in this toggle — then you daze. In thirty seconds, this bulb glows, signaling the success and completion of the treatment. Then I reverse the manipulation, and you arise a creature of renewed sanity."

Guyal looked at Shierl. "Did you hear and comprehend?"

"Yes, Guyal," in a small voice.

"Remember." Then to the Curator: "Marvellous. But how must I sit?"

"Merely relax in the seat. Then I pull the hood slightly forward, to shield the eyes from distraction."

Guyal leaned forward, peered gingerly into the hood. "I fear I do not understand."

The Curator hopped forward impatiently. "It is an act of the utmost facility. Like this." He sat in the chair.

"And how will the hood be applied?"

"In this wise." Kerlin seized a handle, pulled the shield over his face.

"Quick," said Guyal to Shierl. She sprang to the lectern; Kerlin the Curator made a motion to release the hood; Guyal seized the spindly frame, held it. Shierl flung the switches; the Curator relaxed, sighed.

Shierl gazed at Guyal, dark eyes wide and liquid as the great water-flamerian of South Almery. "Is he — dead?"

"I hope not."

They gazed uncertainly at the relaxed form. Seconds passed.

A clanging noise sounded from afar — a crush, a wrench, an exultant bellow, lesser halloos of wild triumph.

Guyal rushed to the door. Prancing, wavering, sidling into the gallery came a multitude of ghosts; through the open door behind, Guyal could see the great head. It was shoving out, pushing into the room. Great ears appeared, part of a bull-neck, wreathed with purple wattles. The wall cracked, sagged, crumbled. A great hand thrust through, a forearm...

Shierl screamed. Guyal, pale and quivering, slammed the door in the face of the nearest ghost. It seeped in around the jamb, slowly, wisp by wisp.

Guyal sprang to the lectern. The bulb showed dullness. Guyal's hands twitched along the controls. "Only Kerlin's awareness controls the magic of the baton," he panted. "So much is clear." He stared into the bulb with agonized urgency. "Glow, bulb, glow…"

By the door the ghost seeped and billowed.

"Glow, bulb, glow…"

The bulb glowed. With a sharp cry Guyal returned the switches to neutrality, jumped down, flung up the hood.

Kerlin the Curator sat looking at him.

Behind the ghost formed itself — a tall white thing in white robes, and the dark eye-holes stared like outlets into non-imagination.

Kerlin the Curator sat looking.

The ghost moved under the robes. A hand like a bird's foot appeared, holding a clod of dingy matter. The ghost cast the matter to the floor; it exploded into a puff of black dust. The motes of the cloud grew, became a myriad of wriggling insects. With one accord they darted across the floor, growing as they spread, and became scuttling creatures with monkey-heads.

Kerlin the Curator moved. "Baton," he said. He held up his hand. It held his baton. The baton spat an orange gout — red dust. It puffed before the rushing horde and each mote became a red scorpion. So ensued a ferocious battle; and little shrieks and chittering sounds rose from the floor.

The monkey-headed things were killed, routed. The ghost sighed, moved his claw-hand once more. But the baton spat forth a ray of purest light and the ghost sloughed into nothingness.

"Kerlin!" cried Guyal. "The demon is breaking into the gallery."

Kerlin flung open the door, stepped forth.

"Baton," said Kerlin, "perform thy utmost intent."

The demon said, "No, Kerlin, hold the magic; I thought you dazed. Now I retreat."

With a vast quaking and heaving he pulled back until once more only his face showed through the hole.

"Baton," said Kerlin, "be you on guard."

The baton disappeared from his hand.

Kerlin turned and faced Guyal and Shierl.

"There is need for many words, for now I die. I die, and the Museum shall lie alone. So let us speak quickly, quickly, quickly..."

Kerlin moved with feeble steps to a portal which snapped aside as he approached. Guyal and Shierl, speculating on the probable trends of Kerlin's disposition, stood hesitantly to the rear.

"Come, come," said Kerlin in sharp impatience. "My strength flags, I die. You have been my death."

Guyal moved slowly forward, with Shierl half a pace behind. Suitable response to the accusation escaped him; words seemed without conviction.

Kerlin surveyed them with a thin grin. "Halt your misgivings and hasten; the necessities to be accomplished in the time available thereto make the task like trying to write the Tomes of Kae in a minim of ink. I wane; my pulsing comes in shallow tides, my sight flickers..."

He waved a despairing hand, then, turning, led them into the inner chamber, where he slumped into a great chair. With many uneasy glances at the door, Guyal and Shierl settled upon a padded couch.

Kerlin jeered in a feeble voice, "You fear the white phantasms? Poh, they are pent from the gallery by the baton, which contains their every effort. Only when I am smitten out of mind — or dead — will the baton cease its function. You must know," he added with somewhat more vigor, "that the energies and dynamics do not channel from my brain but from the central potentium of the Museum, which is perpetual; I merely direct and order the rod."

"But this demon — who or what is he? Why does he come to look through the walls?"

Kerlin's face settled into a bleak mask. "He is Blikdak, Ruler-Divinity of the demon-world Jeldred. He wrenched the hole intent on gulfing the knowledge of the Museum into his mind, but I forestalled him; so he sits waiting in the hole till I die. Then he will glut himself with erudition to the great disadvantage of men."

"Why cannot this demon be exhorted hence and the hole abolished?"

Kerlin the Curator shook his head. "The fires and furious powers I control are not valid in the air of the demon-world, where substance and form are of different entity. So far as you see him, he has brought his environment with him; so far he is safe. When he ventures further into the Museum, the power of Earth dissolves the Jeldred mode; then may I spray him with prismatic fervor from the potentium... But stay, enough of Blikdak for the nonce; tell me, who are you, why are you ventured here, and what is the news of Thorsingol?"

Guyal said in a halting voice, "Thorsingol is passed beyond memory. There is naught above but arid tundra and the old town of the Saponids. I am of the southland; I have coursed many leagues so that I might speak to you and fill my mind with knowledge. This girl Shierl is of the Saponids, and victim of an ancient custom which sends beauty into the Museum at the behest of Blikdak's ghosts."

"Ah," breathed Kerlin, "have I been so aimless? I recall these youthful shapes which Blikdak employed to relieve the tedium of his vigil... They flit down my memory like may-flies along a panel of glass... I put them aside as creatures of his own conception, postulated by his own imagery..."

Shierl shrugged in bewilderment. "But why? What use to him are human creatures?"

Kerlin said dully, "Girl, you are all charm and freshness; the monstrous urges of the demon-lord Blikdak are past your conceiving. These youths of both sexes are his play, on whom he practices various junctures, joinings, coiti, perversions, sadisms, nauseas, antics and at last struggles to the death. Then he sends forth a ghost demanding further youth and beauty."

Shierl whispered, "This was to have been I..."

Guyal said in puzzlement, "I cannot understand. Such acts, in my understanding, are the characteristic derangements of humanity. They are anthropoid by the very nature of the functioning sacs, glands and organs. Since Blikdak is a demon..."

"Consider him!" spoke Kerlin. "His lineaments, his apparatus. He is nothing else but anthropoid, and such is his origin, together with all the demons, frits and winged glowing-eyed creatures that infest latter-day Earth. Blikdak, like the others, is from the mind of man. The sweaty condensation, the stench and vileness, the cloacal humors, the brutal delights, the rapes and sodomies, the scatophiliac whims, the manifold tittering lubricities that have drained through humanity formed a vast tumor; so Blikdak assumed his being, so now this is he. You have seen how he molds his being, so he performs his enjoyments. But of Blikdak, enough. I die, I die!" He sank into the chair with heaving chest.

"See me! My eyes vary and waver. My breath is shallow as a bird's, my bones are the pith of an old vine. I have lived beyond knowledge; in my madness I knew no passage of time. Where there is no knowledge there are no somatic consequences. Now I remember the years and centuries, the millennia, the epochs — they are like quick glimpses through a shutter. So, curing my madness, you have killed me."

Shierl blinked, drew back. "But when you die? What then? Blikdak…"

Guyal asked, "In the Museum of Man is there no knowledge of the exorcisms necessary to dissolve this demon? He is clearly our first antagonist, our immediacy."

"Blikdak must be eradicated," said Kerlin. "Then will I die in ease; then must you assume the care of the Museum." He licked his white lips. "An ancient principle specifies that, in order to destroy a substance, the nature of the substance must be determined. In short, before Blikdak may be dissolved, we must discover his elemental nature." And his eyes moved glassily to Guyal.

"Your pronouncement is sound beyond argument," admitted Guyal, "but how may this be accomplished? Blikdak will never allow such an investigation."

"No; there must be subterfuge, some instrumentality…"

"The ghosts are part of Blikdak's stuff?"

"Indeed."

"Can the ghosts be stayed and prevented?"

"Indeed; in a box of light, the which I can effect by a thought. Yes, a ghost we must have." Kerlin raised his head. "Baton! one ghost; admit a ghost!"

A moment passed; Kerlin held up his hand. There was a faint scratch at the door, and a soft whine could be heard without. "Open," said a voice, full of sobs and catches and quavers. "Open and let forth the youthful creatures to Blikdak. He finds boredom and lassitude in his vigil; so let the two come forth to negate his unease."

Kerlin laboriously rose to his feet. "It is done."

From behind the door came a sad voice, "I am pent, I am snared in scorching brilliance!"

"Now we discover," said Guyal. "What dissolves the ghost dissolves Blikdak."

"True indeed," assented Kerlin.

"Why not light?" inquired Shierl. "Light parts the fabric of the ghosts like a gust of wind tatters the fog."

"But merely for their fragility; Blikdak is harsh and solid, and can withstand the fiercest radiance safe in his demon-land alcove." And Kerlin mused. After a moment he gestured to the door. "We go to the image-expander; there we will explode the ghost to macroid dimension; so shall we find his basis. Guyal of Sfere, you must support my frailness; in truth my limbs are weak as wax."

On Guyal's arm he tottered forward, and with Shierl close at their heels they gained the gallery. Here the ghost wept in its cage of light, and searched constantly for a dark aperture to seep his essence through.

Paying him no heed Kerlin hobbled and limped across the gallery. In their wake followed the box of light and perforce the ghost.

"Open the great door," cried Kerlin in a voice beset with cracking and hoarseness. "The great door into the Cognative Repository!"

Shierl ran ahead and thrust her force against the door; it slid aside, and they looked into the great dark hall, and the golden light from the gallery dwindled into the shadows and was lost.

"Call for Lumen," Kerlin said.

"Lumen!" cried Guyal. "Lumen, attend!"

Light came to the great hall, and it proved so tall that the pilasters along the wall dwindled to threads, and so long and wide that a man might be winded to fatigue in running a dimension. Spaced in equal rows were the black cases with the copper bosses that Guyal and Shierl had noted on their entry. And above each hung five similar cases, precisely fixed, floating without support.

"What are these?" asked Guyal in wonder.

"Would my poor brain encompassed a hundredth part of what these banks know," panted Kerlin. "They are great brains crammed with all that is known, experienced, achieved, or recorded by man. Here is all the lost lore, early and late, the fabulous imaginings, the history of ten million cities, beginnings of time and the presumed finalities; the reason for human existence and the reason for the reason. Daily I have labored and toiled in these banks; my achievement has been a synopsis of the most superficial sort: a panorama across a wide and multifarious country."

Said Shierl, "Would not the craft to destroy Blikdak be contained here?"

"Indeed, indeed; our task would be merely to find the information. Under which casing would we search? Consider these categories: Demonlands; Killings and Mortefactions; Expositions and Dissolutions of Evil; History of Granvilunde (where such an entity was repelled); Attractive and Detractive Hyperordnets; Therapy for Hallucinants and Ghost-takers; Constructive Journal, item for regeneration of burst walls, sub-division for invasion by demons; Procedural Suggestions in Time of Risk… Aye, these and a thousand more. Somewhere is knowledge of how to smite Blikdak's abhorred face back into his quasiplace. But where to look? There is no Index Major; none except the poor synopsis of my compilation. He who seeks specific knowledge must often go on an extended search…" His voice trailed off. Then: "Forward! Forward through the banks to the Mechanismus."

So through the banks they went, like roaches in a maze, and behind drifted the cage of light with the wailing ghost. At last they entered a chamber smelling of metal; again Kerlin instructed Guyal and Guyal called, "Attend us, Lumen, attend!"

Through intricate devices walked the three, Guyal lost and rapt beyond inquiry, even though his brain ached with the want of knowing.

At a tall booth Kerlin halted the cage of light. A pane of vitrean dropped before the ghost. "Observe now," Kerlin said, and manipulated the activants.

They saw the ghost, depicted and projected: the flowing robe, the haggard visage. The face grew large, flattened; a segment under the vacant eye became a scabrous white place. It separated into pustules, and a single pustule swelled to fill the pane. The crater of the pustule was an intricate stippled surface, a mesh as of fabric, knit in a lacy pattern.

"Behold!" said Shierl. "He is a thing woven as if by thread."

Guyal turned eagerly to Kerlin; Kerlin raised a finger for silence. "Indeed, indeed, a goodly thought, especially since here beside us is a rotor of extreme swiftness, used in reeling the cognitive filaments of the cases... Now then observe: I reach to this panel, I select a mesh, I withdraw a thread, and note! The meshes ravel and loosen and part. And now to the bobbin on the rotor, and I wrap the thread, and now with a twist we have the cincture made..."

Shierl said dubiously, "Does not the ghost observe and note your doing?"

"By no means," asserted Kerlin. "The pane of vitrean shields our actions; he is too exercised to attend. And now I dissolve the cage and he is free."

The ghost wandered forth, cringing from the light.

"Go!" cried Kerlin. "Back to your genetrix; back, return and go!"

The ghost departed. Kerlin said to Guyal, "Follow; find when Blikdak snuffs him up."

Guyal at a cautious distance watched the ghost seep up into the black nostril, and returned to where Kerlin waited by the rotor. "The ghost has once more become part of Blikdak."

"Now then," said Kerlin, "we cause the rotor to twist, the bobbin to whirl, and we shall observe."

The rotor whirled to a blur; the bobbin (as long as Guyal's arm) became spun with ghost-thread, at first glowing pastel polychrome, then nacre, then fine milk-ivory.

The rotor spun, a million times a minute, and the thread drawn unseen and unknown from Blikdak thickened on the bobbin.

The rotor spun; the bobbin was full — a cylinder shining with glossy silken sheen. Kerlin slowed the rotor; Guyal snapped a new bobbin into place, and the unraveling of Blikdak continued.

Three bobbins — four — five — and Guyal, observing Blikdak from afar, found the giant face quiescent, the mouth working and sucking, creating the clacking sound which had first caused them apprehension.

Eight bobbins. Blikdak opened his eyes, stared in puzzlement around the chamber.

Twelve bobbins: a discolored spot appeared on the sagging cheek, and Blikdak quivered in uneasiness.

Twenty bobbins: the spot spread across Blikdak's visage, across the slanted fore-dome, and his mouth hung lax; he hissed and fretted.

Thirty bobbins: Blikdak's head seemed stale and putrid; the gun-metal sheen had become an angry maroon, the eyes bulged, the mouth hung open, the tongue lolled limp.

Fifty bobbins: Blikdak collapsed. His dome lowered against the febrile mouth; his eyes shone like feverish coals.

Sixty bobbins: Blikdak was no more.

And with the dissolution of Blikdak so dissolved Jeldred, the demonland created for the housing of evil. The breach in the wall gave on barren rock, unbroken and rigid.

And in the Mechanismus sixty shining bobbins lay stacked neat; the evil so disorganized glowed with purity and iridescence.

Kerlin fell back against the wall. "I expire; my time has come. I have guarded well the Museum; together we have won it away from Blikdak... Attend me now. Into your hands I pass the curacy; now the Museum is your charge to guard and preserve."

"For what end?" asked Shierl. "Earth expires, almost as you... Wherefore knowledge?"

"More now than ever," gasped Kerlin. "Attend: the stars are bright, the stars are fair; the banks know blessed magic to fleet you to youthful climes. Now — I go. I die."

"Wait!" cried Guyal. "Wait, I beseech!"

"Why wait?" whispered Kerlin. "The way to peace is on me; you call me back?"

"How do I extract from the banks?"

"The key to the index is in my chambers, the index of my life..." And Kerlin died.

Guyal and Shierl climbed to the upper ways and stood outside the portal on the ancient flagged floor. It was night; the marble shone faintly underfoot, the broken columns loomed on the sky.

Across the plain the yellow lights of Saponce shone warm through the trees; above in the sky shone the stars.

Guyal said to Shierl, "There is your home; there is Saponce. Do you wish to return?"

She shook her head. "Together we have looked through the eyes of knowledge. We have seen old Thorsingol, and the Sherrit Empire before it, and Golwan Andra before that and the Forty Kades even before. We have seen the warlike green-men, and the knowledgeable Pharials and the Clambs who departed Earth for the stars, as did the Merioneth before them and the Gray Sorcerers still earlier. We have seen oceans rise and fall, the mountains crust up, peak and melt in the beat of rain; we have looked on the sun when it glowed hot and full and yellow… No, Guyal, there is no place for me at Saponce…"

Guyal, leaning back on the weathered pillar, looked up to the stars. "Knowledge is ours, Shierl — all of knowing to our call. And what shall we do?"

Together they looked up to the white stars.

"What shall we do…"

About the Author

Jack Vance was born in 1916 to a well-off California family that, as his childhood ended, fell upon hard times. As a young man he worked at a series of unsatisfying jobs before studying mining engineering, physics, journalism and English at the University of California Berkeley. Leaving school as America was going to war, he found a place as an ordinary seaman in the merchant marine. Later he worked as a rigger, surveyor, ceramicist, and carpenter before his steady production of sf, mystery novels, and short stories established him as a full-time writer.

His output over more than sixty years was prodigious and won him three Hugo Awards, a Nebula Award, a World Fantasy Award for lifetime achievement, as well as an Edgar from the Mystery Writers of America. The Science Fiction and Fantasy Writers of America named him a grandmaster and he was inducted into the Science Fiction Hall of Fame.

His works crossed genre boundaries, from dark fantasies (including the highly influential *Dying Earth* cycle of novels) to interstellar space operas, from heroic fantasy (the *Lyonesse* trilogy) to murder mysteries featuring a sheriff (the Joe Bain novels) in a rural California county. A Vance story often centered on a competent male protagonist thrust into a dangerous, evolving situation on a planet where adventure was his daily fare, or featured a young person setting out on a perilous odyssey over difficult terrain populated by entrenched, scheming enemies.

Late in his life, a world-spanning assemblage of Vance aficionados came together to return his works to their original form, restoring material cut by editors whose chief preoccupation was the page count of a pulp magazine. The result was the complete and authoritative *Vance Integral Edition* in 44 hardcover volumes. Spatterlight Press is now publishing the VIE texts as ebooks, and as print-on-demand paperbacks.

Colophon

This book was printed using Adobe Arno Pro as the primary text font.

This title was created from the digital archive of the Vance Integral Edition, a series of 44 books produced under the aegis of the author by a worldwide group of his readers. The VIE project gratefully acknowledges the editorial guidance of Norma Vance, as well as the cooperation of the Department of Special Collections at Boston University, whose John Holbrook Vance collection has been an important source of textual evidence.

Special thanks to R.C. Lacovara, Patrick Dusoulier, Koen Vyverman, Paul Rhoads, Chuck King, Gregory Hansen, Suan Yong, and Josh Geller for their invaluable assistance preparing final versions of the source files.

Digitize: Donna Adams, Paul Rhoads; Format: R.C. Lacovara, Tim Stretton; Diff: Damien G. Jones, Tim Stretton; Tech Proof: Errico Rescigno; Text Integrity: Paul Rhoads, Steve Sherman, Tim Stretton; Implement: Donna Adams, Mike Dennison; Security: Paul Rhoads, Compose: Joel Anderson, John A. Schwab; Comp Review: John A. D. Foley, Andreas Irle, Charles King, Stephane Leibovitsch, Robin L. Rouch; Update Verify: Paul Rhoads; Textport: Patrick Dusoulier, Charles King; Proofread: Mike Barrett, Richard Behrens, Patrick Dymond, Charles King, David Mortimore, David Reitsema, Bill Schaub, Gabriel Stein

Artwork (maps based on original drawings by Jack and Norma Vance):

Paul Rhoads, Christopher Wood

Book Design: Joel Anderson

Proofing: Christian J. Corley, Steve Sherman

Jacket Blurb: Matt Hughes

Management: John Vance, Koen Vyverman

Printed in Great Britain
by Amazon

9a57c3bb-10be-4642-8fcc-4508bf61cd9aR02